Dragon Tamer

By Kathleen Scott

On the tropical island paradise of Cambry, a ghastly, flesh-eating blight is killing the dragons and threatening prime hatching grounds.

Desperate to protect his beloved creatures, hatchery director Darion Archer calls on the International Field Marshall service to help investigate the outbreak and see an end to this blight. When beautiful IFM agent Serrah Gayle arrives, he is unprepared for his attraction to her—and for the fact that she has a fear of dragons.

Serrah has double trouble, fighting her fear of dragons and her attraction to their sexy keeper. Yet to save these legendary creatures, she must face down that fear and draw on the power of Darion's love.

They can only hope it is not too late.

Warning, this title contains the following: explicit sex, graphic language.

Hard to Guard

By Nina Mamone

Two guardians + long-denied passion + a quest to recover a kidnapped wyrm = spontaneous combustion

A construction worker by day, a Guardian by night, Connor has had it with the irresponsible antics of the wyrms he vowed to keep secret from the human world. The only reason he keeps going is to be near the sassy, sexy, but totally out-of-his-league Sorcha. However, for the past five years, Sorcha's not-so-subtle digs have convinced him that she only sees him as a stuffy, wet blanket.

Sorcha lusts after Connor and may even love him. But after five years of poking, prodding, teasing—anything to get some kind of reaction, even a frown—she's given up hope of having a relationship with him. He has made it very clear that working with her to find a kidnapped wyrm is the very last thing he wants to do.

An unaccounted-for wyrm is a deadly wild card, and after a dangerous aphrodisiac appears on the streets, Sorcha and Connor will have to join forces to ensure the safety of everyone they care about.

Warning, this title contains the following: explicit sex, graphic language, violence, narcissistic wyrms.

I Dream of Dragons II

Kathleen Scott
Nina Mamone

A Samhain Publishing, Ltd. publication.

Samhain Publishing, Ltd.
577 Mulberry Street, Suite 1520
Macon, GA 31201
www.samhainpublishing.com

I Dream of Dragons II
Print ISBN: 1-59998-365-6

Editing by Angela James
Cover by Anne Cain & Scott Carpenter

Dragon Tamer
First Samhain Publishing, Ltd. electronic publication: September 2007
Hard to Guard
First Samhain Publishing, Ltd. electronic publication: September 2007
First Samhain Publishing, Ltd. print publication: March 2008

Contents

Dragon Tamer

Kathleen Scott

Dedication

For all the dragons and the people who dream of them.

Chapter One

The stench of rotting scales sucked all the breathable air from the lair. Darion pulled his thick homespun vest up to cover his nose and mouth to block as much of the putrid smell as possible. Opening his mouth didn't help, it only made the taste stick to his tongue.

His assistants, Ontonio and Palmer, held torches aloft lighting their way through the dark cave. The flames danced off crystals imbedded in the rock, giving the interior a shimmery fairytale quality incongruous with the death he knew they'd find.

Darion locked his jaws together. Pain burned in his chest and eyes.

A sharp incline in the cave floor sent the party down into the lower chamber. He knew this lair as he knew the layout of his own suite. This was Sorcha's cave. It had been over a week since he'd last seen the big, beautiful Amethyst dragon take flight. Not unusual during nesting season, but with the blight that plagued the dragon population of late, Darion didn't want to take any chances with his flock.

Judging from the smell, he was too late.

Where could the blight have come from? Six months ago the entire adult female dragon population of Cambry was alive and healthy. Now, as they came nearer to the central chamber, Darion doubted they would find Sorcha alive.

The ramp ended and opened into a huge room with a ceiling that spiraled upward, nearly hollowing out the interior of Mount Crag. Sorcha lay curled in the center of the sand pit. She raised her head and sent a low resonant whine echoing through the lair.

"It's all right, my love. It's Darion." The perfect acoustics of the chamber amplified the sorrow in his voice. Gods, he wanted to hide that from her. She'd be scared if she knew he was hurting.

The large jewel-like eyes had turned to a milky white, the blight having stolen her sight.

She lifted her once-proud head and sniffed the air, trying to locate Darion in her blindness. Disregarding the foul odor emanating from the dragon's flesh, he hurried to her.

"You're not alone, dear girl." He ran his hand down her long nose, then rubbed the spot between her eyes that made her preen and purr. Her eyes slid closed and the whine turned to a near sob.

She pulled her head from his hands and turned as if to look over her shoulder. At first he thought she wanted to know who was in the chamber with him, but Ontonio and Palmer were standing behind him, not in front where she indicated. Another low moan rumbled through Sorcha's diseased body. Her massive tail whipped in a lazy arc. Five blue and purple eggs lay protected by the curve of her body in the warm sand of the lair.

"Eggs," he breathed. Even with Sorcha's death only moments away, he still had a chance to save her babies. "You want me to take your eggs?"

She gave a mournful trill.

He motioned for Ontonio and Palmer to gather the eggs, about the size of a large loaf of bread, and put them in their packs. With any luck the tiny dragons inside were still viable. Darion had no way to know if the blight could infect the reproductive process. Could the bacteria—or whatever it was—cross the soft membrane of the shells before they left the body? Or had the male dragons passed it on during the mating flight?

Gods, there was just no way to know at this point. And it killed him.

"Take the eggs and start back. I'm going to stay here with Sorcha."

He took a seat in the soft sand and let her rest her weary head in his lap. Without thought he began to stroke the ridge of her eye and the soft spot directly behind her ear. A low contented hum came from her throat. Her sides billowed with each breath. Ragged scales fluttered with every movement. The disease had ravaged her so quickly. She hadn't looked like this the last time he'd seen her. She'd been healthy and strong with a brilliant purple sheen that designated her as an Amethyst.

Darion didn't know how long he sat there holding onto Sorcha and crooning loving words into her ears, but he would forever remember the last shuddery breath she took. And the moment he felt her incredible spirit leave her body.

He walked from the lair into the fading light towards the settlement surrounded by the music of the dragons' dirge. With each step he vowed to find the source of the blight, if it took him until his own spirit left his body.

Chapter Two

Serrah stepped off the shuttle and shoved her sunglasses on her nose. Damn, no one warned her Cambry sunshine could blind a person. What with the towering white crystal spires of the central coliseum and the reflection of the emerald seas surrounding the island, it was any wonder the natives had any *retina* left.

She walked down the main concourse of the shuttle station and waited with the rest of the travelers to pick up her luggage. When the call had come for an investigator, she'd had no idea the nature of the problem. Normal procedure called for the complaint to go to review before an agent was sent into the field to gather data to determine if a formal investigation was even warranted. Her superiors had waived the red tape and given her a shuttle pass leaving that afternoon.

After seventeen hours aboard a shuttle with honeymooning couples and students on holiday, she couldn't wait to get to work. Too many happy people in close quarters tended to make her nervous. They had no idea what the real world was like and she hadn't been able to do even a preliminary survey on the case to drown out their excited voices.

The file uploaded onto her handheld hadn't given her much information on what exactly the case entailed. Normally, her jurisdiction included illegal shipping, black market goods, bootlegging and drug trafficking. Looking around at the pristine paradise before her, she could very well imagine Cambry could be a haven for all those activities.

As far as she was concerned everyone was a suspect, and everyone had something to hide.

However, everyone knew that the island of Cambry was famous for its dragons. The very thought made her shudder.

She glanced at her watch as the luggage began its slow jaunt around the carousel. Her lonely bag sat like a black splotch among the colorful pieces packed by vacationers. It stood out for both its official capacity and unimaginative design.

Serrah threw her shoulders back and walked to retrieve her bag. She slung her briefcase higher on the other shoulder and turned towards the passenger pick-up. Someone from Calusia settlement had the dubious honor of picking her up, though she hadn't been given a contact name or description. Neither of which made a seasoned agent such as herself very comfortable with the situation. Even a small scrap of information from her supervisor would have been preferable than going into an unknown blind.

A tall man stood alone at the end of the walkway, hands folded behind his back, scanning the crowd for someone. The outfit he wore looked more like glorified pajamas than actual daywear. Loose twill pants tied at his trim waist were topped with a gauzy vest he had buttoned up, but wore without a shirt underneath. Muscular arms were clasped behind his back in a deceptively casual pose as he watched people leaving the shuttle port.

Her gaze was drawn to him, not just for the unusual way he dressed, but because there was something otherworldly in his presence. Sorrow hung about his shoulders like a rough-hewn cloak. He wore no sunshades.

Eyes the same color as the lagoon that flanked the Kella City shuttle port turned on her.

He stepped forward and bowed. "Agent Gayle?"

Serrah nodded. At least he seemed formal and respectful. She didn't always get such a greeting. People were usually not eager to make her acquaintance. "And you are?"

"Darion Archer. I run the hatching ground at Calusia settlement."

Hatching ground?

Dragons.

The unease she'd felt before expanded its range to include both her chest and gut.

"Can I take those from you?" He leaned over to take her bags, but she jerked them back from his grasp.

"I can manage, thank you."

He raised a dark brow at her and turned to start out of the terminal. "We have a long ride ahead of us. Do you need food or facilities before we leave?"

"I'm fine."

He walked her out the doors and to a lot where small hover cars and larger drone buses stood waiting for passengers.

"I'm sorry we don't have better transportation, but the settlement is in the foothills of the Ocher Mountains and the larger shuttles can't navigate there." They ended up at the far end of the lot, standing next to a climb cart. She hadn't seen one of those since she did her undergrad field work in a region off the Mallis Ocean over ten years before. Surely they didn't even make parts for them anymore.

The climb cart was even smaller in size than the hover cars and could fit only two people. A storage bin took up the entire back seat, and a little canopy covered the occupants from the hot sun.

He opened the storage compartment for her. "You can put your things in here. They'll be safer than letting them bounce around in the seat with you."

This assignment had ominous written all over it. Hatching grounds. Climb carts. A driver who looked good enough to eat and even better to arrest. So far nothing added up to a case that should have even landed in her assignment file. At least nothing that her superiors knew about.

Serrah climbed into the seat and strapped the harness over her shoulder. Darion sat behind the controls and didn't bother to strap himself to the seat. Maybe the ancient bucket of bolts couldn't achieve lift-off, or didn't go faster than a brisk walk. Either way she felt a little foolish now for having put on her own harness.

He looked over at her with those lagoon eyes and an amused smile curled the corner of his mouth. "Don't worry, you won't fall out."

Crap, now she had to keep the damn thing buckled or look like a complete moron. "Yeah, well, I don't know your driving record. I'm not taking any chances."

"I'll get you there in one piece. Beyond that, I don't offer any guarantees."

She couldn't decide if it was a joke or a warning.

The car came to life and the lift-off proved smooth, if not very high off the ground. No wonder he said they would be traveling for a while, at only a foot off the road they were inhibited by having to follow the curvature of the ground. Not a good sign.

"Do you want to tell me why I was brought here to Cambry and what the director of a hatching ground would need with an International Field Marshall?"

"You don't know?"

"I wouldn't have asked the question if I knew the answer."

He made a face and looked out the wind screen. "The dragons are dying. There's a blight killing them. Rots their scales right off and eats the underflesh while they're still alive. It works its way down into their organs, attacks their respiratory systems until they slowly suffocate."

Serrah stared at him. The dragons dying? Why was this the first she'd heard of it? A blight of such magnitude should have been carried by all the major news agencies. Still... "Sounds like you need a biologist that specializes in draconic physiology and disease, not an IFM agent."

"We did call one in. He was less than helpful."

"I'll need to see any reports he made. Any information at all that shows this case falls into my jurisdiction." Even if it didn't, the ramifications of widespread dragon deaths would have far-reaching effects.

She brushed her hair back from her face as Archer pushed the throttle forward and their speed increased. His dark sable hair was cut in a rather haphazard fashion, but somehow it fit the rugged look of him. It wasn't long enough to blow into his eyes, but every once in a while he'd shake his head to clear it from his cheeks.

His skin was a deep bronze from—she guessed—spending so much time out in the heat and sun. Darion Archer was a broad-shouldered man with long legs and muscular arms. He was about as fit a specimen of manhood as she'd ever seen, but then working with dragons on a daily basis he would have to be. It was a job not for the faint of heart or body.

Serrah shook her head, trying not to think about the dragons or the past she kept buried. There was no way the IFM had discovered her little secret and sent her here to use it. She doubted her talent would even be useful in an investigation. No, they'd probably sent her because of her expertise in uncovering conspiracies and following credit cues back to the big bosses. The question was: How would killing off the dragons benefit anyone?

She pulled her handheld from her belt harness and started looking for any and all information she could find on the island paradise and resort of Cambry.

Chapter Three

Whatever Darion had been expecting when he contacted his brother in the IFM, it hadn't been Agent Serrah Gayle. Perhaps he was out of touch, but he thought women were supposed to be loving and nurturing. So far Agent Gayle was nothing more than a badge with boobs and an attitude. Nice boobs though they were. It wasn't his fault her superiors didn't share with her the dire circumstances of the "case".

Gods, did she actually call it "a case"?

It was so easy to boil a problem down to a label when you weren't the one touched by the pain and agony of the crisis.

He spared a glance at her profile as she tapped away on her handheld. How could such a beautiful woman be so damn cold and unfeeling? They didn't program that into their agents, did they? Sure Tavil had changed when he'd joined the IFM, but Darion had always figured the training had only amplified the quiet inner strength that was inherent in his brother's personality.

She raised a slender arm and brushed pale hair back from a heart-shaped face. She pulled her bottom lip between her teeth as she read whatever was on the small screen in front of her. It seemed like such a vulnerable action for a woman who appeared to be anything but. However, that small unconscious action caused his lower belly to tighten in a kick of unexpected lust.

"Dragons are one of your biggest draws to the island, right?" She looked over at him, but he couldn't see her eyes. She'd had on sunshades since he'd met her at the shuttle port entrance.

"As big a draw as the beaches or volcano spirits." He eased back the directional control as they started up a hill. The climb cart's mercurial engine decided to take the opportunity to begin to chug and sputter as if the climb were too much for it to manage.

Agent Gayle shot him a look over the top of her glasses. He didn't take his attention from the road to give her more than a cursory glance, though he really wanted to study her in much closer circumstances. "Are we even going to make it to the settlement?"

"We'll make it."

No doubt Agent Gayle wasn't used to the rustic surroundings of the settlement. Dragon care and maintenance didn't require legions of electronic devices. Low-tech equipment usually did the best job and had been proven ever since man and dragon had formed their first bonds. That wasn't to say the settlement lacked modern conveniences—they just didn't rely on such things for everyday tasks dealing with the dragons. Records keeping was another matter.

Damn, he wished Mercia, his office assistant, wasn't off visiting her family. He relied on her to keep things running smoothly and they hadn't been since she'd left a week ago. He'd hoped Tavil would be sent home, or he'd had more time to prepare for Agent Gayle's arrival. When the call came earlier in the day to meet the IFM agent, the entire settlement had fallen into chaos to prepare. Thank the gods for Ontonio and Palmer.

The land inclined sharply. With slow, painful progress, the climb cart lurched forward as if the very gravity beneath them thickened and pulled at the cart like quicksand. The thrusters were failing and failing fast.

Damn! He shouldn't have spoken so soon. Once the thrusters were gone they'd end up having to walk the rest of the way up the foothills.

"It's still not too late to turn around and go back for a rental." Agent Gayle sounded helpful, if not a little uncertain.

Darion shifted into a lower gear. They barely stayed afloat over the ground surface, but at least they were moving. Unfortunately, the lower gear didn't allow for a great amount of speed.

From the corner of his eyes he caught the subtle shake of her head. She went back to her handheld and left her disgruntled words unspoken. Small favors. For once since the dragons began dying off, Darion felt like something had actually gone his way. If she had turned to him and started complaining, he'd have dropped the climb cart and forced her to walk on principle alone. Just the thought made him smile. Somehow the image of her getting all hot and sweaty trekking through the jungle was very tempting. She'd look even more tempting than she did now. If that were possible.

He glanced over at her as she straightened in her seat and looked over at Darion. Dark pink lips were parted on a silent question.

"What?"

"According to your Chamber of Commerce, sloughed dragon scales are Cambry's biggest source of export." The statistic came out like an accusation.

"Not for long."

"No, that's my point. The question I need to answer is who or what would benefit in the loss of the dragon population."

Darion frowned as the climb cart gave an exhausted belch and chug. "No one will benefit."

"Someone has to. Why kill them off, if not for profit?"

Did her world involve so many conspiracies and machinations that the thought something could be a purely biological component sound far-fetched to her? Granted, Darion had been the one to call the IFM in to investigate, but he'd mistakenly thought his brother would arrive and request a team of scientists to discover the reason for the dragons' deaths, not a stun-rod toting militant female who made his blood boil. "There was no evidence to support that the blight is anything other than some nasty dragon-flesh eating bacteria of unknown origin."

"Like I said, I want to see the data your expert collected."

She was also suspicious.

"I'll get everything to your hut when we arrive."

"If we arrive," she muttered under her breath and turned her attention back to the small screen in front of her.

With a violent jerk, the climb cart hit the ground. The thrusters hissed and popped, straining to lift, but to no avail. They were dead on the ground.

Darion killed power to the engines and turned to Agent Gayle, who looked at him over her sunshades as if she wanted to commit murder. "I'll get your bags out of the back."

"You're kidding, right?"

"Not unless you want to sit here in the blazing sun and wait for help to arrive." A little thrill went through his body as she unhooked the harness and climbed out of the passenger seat. Aggravating her proved to be very enjoyable.

He opened the storage compartment so she could grab her bags. She nudged him with her shoulder to move him out of the way. It was hard for him to stand there and not help her with her bags. She didn't seem as if she wanted anything to do with him giving her a hand with whatever precious possessions she carried in her luggage. And yet, he found himself wildly attracted to her for some reason.

Darion started walking up the incline to the lower range of foothills. He let his glance slide over his reluctant companion. She looked fit enough, maybe he wouldn't end up carrying her at some point. But he couldn't help but dig at her. "The walk from here is pretty grueling. If you need to stop and rest, let me know."

She readjusted the straps of her larger case and configured them to wear as a backpack. "Same goes."

A smile tugged the side of his mouth. The woman was all grit and sass. Wait until she came face to face with a full-grown king Ruby. They were the largest dragons on the island and they didn't suffer fools or arrogance lightly. "Let's get walking then."

Agent Gayle raised her arm. "After you, Archer."

Chapter Four

The sun began to slide down the horizon as they made the outskirts of the settlement. Exhaustion hung on Serrah heavier than her luggage, but she'd be damned before she'd let Darion Archer know she longed for a comfortable bed and a cool shower.

Comfort wasn't something she expected on her cases. The IFM often sent her to areas that seemed to be stuck in some bubble of time, untouched by the modern world, but she usually didn't have to hike up a mountain carrying thirty pounds of clothes and equipment on her back. She usually didn't feel compelled to hide her discomfort from her contact person. She couldn't help but feel that she was being tested for some reason.

As they entered the gates of the settlement proper, two young men approached, as different in appearance as any two people could be and remain a member of the same species. One, short and stocky, with a round head and short neck, looked like he could carry an adolescent dragon on his back and not break a sweat or strain a muscle. The other youth was tall; his long blond hair sported beaded braids at his temples.

As they neared, the blond said, "Where have you been? We've been trying to raise you on your radio."

Archer shrugged. "Thrusters died. We had to walk."

The men exchanged looks and kept quiet. Serrah had the feeling that Archer could have called the settlement and sent someone for them, but he hadn't. When she'd asked him during the trek, he'd told her there was no other conveyance at the settlement. She'd found it hard to believe at the time. Now, even more so.

"Palmer, Ontonio this is Agent Gayle from the IFM."

She nodded a greeting to both men.

"They are my chief assistants."

"I'll want to interview them as well as anyone else who has direct daily contact with the dragons."

Archer nodded and put his hand in the tuck of her waist to guide her on. The sudden touch sent an unexpected tingle through her body. She turned and looked at him, but he had cast his eyes forward, unaware of the current he'd let loose in her.

He showed her to a small hut that stood on stilts at the edge of a lush tropical forest. A small porch ran around the outside of the structure where two chairs sat facing an opening in the trees and looked out over a crystal blue cove. The view was breathtaking.

Movement at the edge of the tree line caught her eye as a huge dragon lifted its regal head to look at her. The color matched the foliage so perfectly she hadn't seen it until it moved. Large jewel-like eyes looked into hers.

Serrah swallowed as the gentle brush of the dragon's mind touched her own. The noble creature bowed to her then jumped into the air, taking flight.

Massive leathery wings beat as he became airborne. The dying sun cast a golden glow over the animal, turning the emerald scales to thousands of glittery shards.

"Magnificent." The observation came out on a breathy sigh. She'd been a child the last time she'd seen a dragon take to the air.

When she looked at Archer, he had a sad smile on his handsome face. He watched the great creature grow smaller as it flew into the heart of the Ocher Mountains. "There's nothing like them."

Silence stretched before them, until Archer shook his head and handed her a key chit. "It's programmed for your room and the library center only. Anywhere else you want to go, the records department or hatching ground, you'll have to have an escort."

Serrah closed the chit in her hand. "Is that for all visitors, or just me?"

"It's true for everyone in the settlement other than my staff."

She nodded. At least they were moderately careful on security, but that would only extend to the records and hatching ground. Adult dragons obviously came and went as they pleased and could come into contact with a multitude of variables that could be detrimental to their health. Was there any way to confine or segregate the dragons until the investigation proved what caused the blight? She'd have to find out about that.

"We eat in a communal dining hall." He looked at his watch and then off into the settlement. "About now."

"Let me put my things in my room and we can go." A communal dining hall would give her the perfect opportunity to observe the inhabitants of Calusia settlement and get a feel for the community in general. People often let their guard down while enjoying a casual meal—more so if that meal was a nightly ritual.

She waved the chit before the lock pad and the door clicked open. A rush of cool air from a large ceiling fan came from the room and dried the sweat on her skin. For the first time that day she was glad that she wore a dark shirt in a thick fabric. Her nipples grew hard and she hurried through the door, keeping her back to Archer.

The room was about as basic in function as one could be. A bed took up the middle of the room, covered in a sheer white netting that hung from the ceiling and came down to shield the bed from insects. A desk and chair sat up against the far wall with outlets for her communication devices.

Archer stood in the doorway. "Does the room work for you?"

Serrah let her pack off her shoulders and set it on the floor. Her briefcase she set by the desk. "It's fine. I just need a place to sleep, shower and work."

"Do you need some time to freshen up before we walk to the dining hall?"

She was about to decline but thought better of it. Splashing cool water on her face and washing her hands would probably not be amiss. "I'll meet you in five."

Archer watched her for a moment before he turned and walked outside, closing the door behind him.

She moved to the bathroom, turned on the tap and gathered water in her cupped hands. Her temporal lobe still tingled where the dragon had tried to connect with her. Thank the gods her shields held. The very idea she'd been in such close proximity to intelligent creatures who could talk directly to her telepathically was way too disconcerting for her peace of mind. It was the reason she'd denied the ability for so long—why she'd insisted on a career that took her on a wide circuit away from dragons.

Be that as it may, why had her superiors assigned her this case? She had no real knowledge of draconic physiology, and her employment applications and profile didn't mention her psychic connection with dragons. She'd been very careful her entire life never to discuss the ability.

The last time she'd done so, the Cambrian Dragon Tamers had been to her hometown of Lysca and her father had taken her to the show. She'd been so small, holding onto his hand as they watched the beautiful beasts and their riders perform aerial stunts as the crowd sat awestruck beneath them.

A large Topaz had turned his head and looked at her, and a voice had spoken into her mind. *Pretty child.*

The words had tickled and made her laugh. She turned to her father and said the dragon called her pretty. Her father had taken her from the grounds and made her promise never to talk to the dragons again. The riders would carry her off in the night and she'd never see her family again. At the time she'd believed him.

After that, nights were terrifying for her. She'd sleep with the covers pulled over her little head, afraid the dragons and their riders would pull her from her bed and the safety of her family. Once or twice she'd felt the same ticklish brush of their minds against hers, but she'd close the sensation down tightly and isolate it, keeping them out.

Serrah cupped more water in her hand and patted the back of her neck. How was she supposed to keep those voices out of her head now? There were too many of them.

She grabbed a towel from the rack and dried her face and neck before steeling herself against the mind intrusions to come.

Chapter Five

Darion ushered Agent Gayle into the dining hall. Most diners were finishing their meals. The chatter of conversations ground to a halt when they entered. He'd wondered if curiosity would get the better of them or if they'd be discreet enough to allow him and the agent to eat in relative peace. He couldn't fault them for their undivided attention—the hopes of the entire dragon population may very well fall on the slim but sturdy shoulders of the diminutive member of the IFM.

As they passed the tables, Darion nodded to his friends. The entire human element of Calusia settlement only totaled four hundred when they were staffed to capacity. Needless to say, it was a very small, intimate community.

He grabbed a tray and two plates of supper. "There isn't a lot of choice. We eat what's prepared. It's good and fully nutritious. You do have your choice of beverage." He nodded to a cart where large canisters of varying drinks were kept.

Cool eyes, caught somewhere between a wildflower and an Amethyst's scales, regarded him and then the tray he held. "I'll get the drinks. What are you having?"

"Juice for me, please."

She turned without another word and made her way through the crowded dining hall to the drink cart. The woman walked as if she owned the place. Her shoulders were thrust back, her spine straight. There was no doubt she had been trained by the military or a federal agency. In this case the agency just so happened to be a global one that had expanded its scope to begin policing the space ports for illegal goods and drugs coming onto the planet surface.

An uneasy pang beat low in his heart. Serrah Gayle may be one tough agent, but she looked much too delicate and feminine to hold her own against one of the drug runners that frequented the island.

He waited for her before heading to his usual seat by the window overlooking the northern corner of the settlement. The window faced a waterfall that ran off a high cliff and crashed to the jagged rocks below. The unspoiled beauty of the view never failed to amaze him.

As he watched, an Agate circled the cliff a few times before coming in to perch on the rock cliff. It threw back its large, diamond-shaped head and let out a long mournful trumpet. Darion's blood chilled in his chest. Another dragon had just died and Arcane the Agate released his pain to the world.

The answering cries from the other dragons shook the dining hall.

Agent Gayle set the glass of fruit juice in front of Darion before sliding into a seat across from him. A quick glance to her face showed her smooth features tightened into a mask of stress. She held the glass with tense hands. The knuckles white.

"Agent Gayle?"

"Yes?"

She looked at him as if her reaction was an annoyance. Darion couldn't help but think there was something more to the brackets around her mouth and the stark look that came into her eyes. She looked as if she'd lived around the dragons all her life and knew the cost of even just one dragon death.

"Arcane is singing a lament for one of his dead brethren."

She nodded and picked up her utensils, unrolling her napkin with quick, efficient fingers. "I know."

"It bothers you." He leaned his elbows on the table and studied her over his laced fingers.

"Of course it does. I've been sent here to stop it and a death occurs on the night I arrive. That's one too many."

That was only partially true. Some other reason made her look as if she'd been hit in the gut by her own stun-rod. He doubted very much that it was just the unbearable sadness of the dragon's song. For now, he'd let the explanation go.

"I'll need to go into the mountains tomorrow and find out exactly which dragon passed."

She cocked her head to the side. "You don't know?"

"Not until we check the caves. I've seen previously healthy dragons die within a week or two of contracting the disease. It's hard to be sure which dragon is ill and which is just on a flight somewhere. We have nothing in place to inventory them."

Taking a long slow drink of her water, she watched him over her glass as if she didn't believe him. When she put her drink back down she said, "Why haven't the dragons been tagged?"

Outrage spilled through his veins. He leaned over his plate. "They aren't livestock, Agent Gayle. They're highly intelligent beings who can think circles around humans. Don't even suggest they be humiliated by the indignity of tagging."

"It would be a hell of a lot easier to tag them and know which of them died and where they likely are than wasting valuable time by searching all the caves in these mountains."

People at the tables nearest them started to turn around and listen to the heated conversation. Darion didn't care. Couldn't afford to care. The agent needed to know the reality of working with dragons or she'd be useless to them.

He swung his arm to indicate the dragons outside the window. "But not very practical. Every eighteen months a dragon sheds their complete suit of scales. If we could even manage to gain the dragons' cooperation for such an undertaking, after tracking down every last one, we'd have to repeat the process in a year and a half. How much manpower do you think that would take?"

She pursed her lips and raised a brow as if she'd argue with him, but her face took on that sudden shocky look she'd had when the dragons began their lament.

"You don't look well."

"I'm fine." The words were forced out behind gritted teeth. Her fingers gripped the table so tightly her hands blanched.

"Let me take you back to your hut."

"Not necessary. I can find the way back."

"It might not be necessary, but I'll do it anyhow." He stood and came around to her side of the table and wrapped a hand around her upper arm. Muscles tensed and flexed at his grip. He leaned down to speak close to her ear so those listening failed to hear his words. "I'm the director of a hatching ground where dragons are dying and as such it's my responsibility. I'll be damned before I'll let an IFM agent become ill while in a settlement under my leadership."

The fight seemed to leave her then. She stood under her own steam. "Can I at least take something back to my hut to eat later?"

Darion looked down into her face. He softened his expression and gazed into her incredible eyes. "Of course you can," he said almost in a whisper. "Let me see you back to your hut and I'll bring you some snacks in a little while."

She allowed him to walk her out of the dining hall and across the commons.

Outside, the night air retained some of the humidity from the day. The dragons' mournful cries continued to serenade the moon. The sound vibrated through Darion's body. Worry scored his insides like steel wool. It chafed and hurt. What beautiful beast had lost its life this day? Speculation alone threatened to cripple him.

He walked her up to her door and took the key chit from her hand and waved it over the access pad. "Get some rest. I'll be back later with some food and the reports from the draconic physiologist."

She looked up at him with something akin to confusion. "I've offended you and here you are treating me like I'm the best date you've had this year."

Desire slammed into his sternum like a runaway shuttle. He leaned into her. "With the sad state of affairs around here, you are."

The unexpected happened then. She graced him with a smile. It was rather hesitant and unsure, only moving the corner of her mouth up a fraction. Almost like the action was foreign to her.

Then she stepped over the threshold and closed the door in his face.

Darion stood there for a few moments staring at her door. He couldn't figure her out. Not that he needed to in order for her to work her "case".

He shook his head to clear it and stepped off the porch. First order of business, he needed to go to his office and collect the files for her. Then he had to try and figure out which dragons his team hadn't seen in a week. It wasn't a perfect system, but it was the best they had at the moment.

Agent Gayle's idea for tagging the dragons had merit, though he'd given her hell for it. He and his assistants had discussed it at length in committee, but decided the project would be unfeasible. The dragons wouldn't have enjoyed it either. Quite honestly, there hadn't been a need to move to such drastic measures until a few months ago when the blight began. Since then they'd been trying to come up with measures to make it easier to find the diseased dragons, who hid in their caves to die.

Lanterns were placed around the settlement so those walking after dark could see their way. The golden glow cast long shadows along the even grounds of the commons. He'd walked these paths so many times over the years he could have done it without the lighting, but he couldn't quite stop thinking about how the agent looked as the shadows had accentuated the hollows of her face, giving her an ethereal look.

She'd probably be offended if he told her that seeing her so vulnerable made his protective instincts surface. Somehow he didn't think she'd appreciate it.

He waved his key chit in front of the lock at the administration building. Cool air swirled around him as he moved down the corridor to his office.

This time of night the offices were deserted. Not that many people came into this building. Most of the hatching ground tasks were done in the field at the sand pits. The offices were mostly kept for storage of records and communications purposes.

He opened his office and moved to the filing system. Tapping in the code for the draconic physiologist's files, Darion wondered what Agent Gayle would find in the reports that an entire settlement dedicated to the health and welfare of dragons hadn't.

File not found.

"What?" He retyped the code. His fingers probably slipped on the keys. Understandable since his mind had scattered in about four directions at once.

File not found.

What was he doing wrong? Maybe he had the code wrong to begin with. No matter. He kept a hard copy of the information in the filing cabinet just in case of instances like this. Electronics, just like people, were not infallible.

He rolled the desk chair over to the cabinet and pulled out the drawer where he'd placed the file a few weeks prior. It wasn't where he'd last seen it. Frustrated, he started at the beginning of the files and worked his way through to the back.

Not there.

Where in the hell could it have gone? This was the only drawer he kept hard copies in—the file could be nowhere else in his office. And he'd never taken it to his quarters.

Dread moved through him, but he pushed it away.

In order for both files to be gone, someone within his trusted circle of assistants would have to be responsible for lifting it. If anyone wanted to study the files for legitimate reasons, all they had to do was ask. No one needed to be so clandestine about obtaining them. So what was in the files that would make them important enough to take without asking? Or had Mercia reorganized and not told him of doing so? If so, that still didn't explain why the electronic files were inaccessible. Darion didn't believe in coincidences like that.

He'd received a verbal report from the physiologist along with the written documents. There had been nothing to report. Again, Darion had to ask himself: Why take the file?

There was nothing else for it. He had to let Agent Gayle know his suspicions. No matter the outcome. The fate of the dragons depended on full disclosure.

Chapter Six

Serrah stood with her back to the door, taking a few calming breaths. The damn dragons were inside her head. Their pain and agony reached far into her soul and shook her at the very foundations.

How could the tamers have stood to have another consciousness inside their brain, speaking with them as if the words were part of their own thoughts? No wonder they had been forced to seek refuge on another world. Abilities such as that were not to be trusted. She didn't even trust herself with them. But then her father had made damn sure she never wanted to explore those voices in her head. Fear had made an excellent deterrent.

Well, there would be no rest until the dragons finished their mourning. The song shot through her nervous system like molten rock, filling in the spaces then hardening until she became heavy all over. Her heart was a dead weight in her chest.

She pushed off from the door and began to unpack her communications system. There was a lot of information she'd not been able to dig through before they'd made the settlement. Walking and trying to read the handheld had not been easy on their trek to Calusia and she'd been forced to give up the search. Now there was no reason not to continue.

It took very little time before Serrah sat at her comm station and found the information on Cambrian exports. Dragon scales were a very hot commodity both on world and off. Most industries owed much of their product to some form of refined dragon scales. The uses were many and vast, from textiles to pharmaceuticals. The question was: Which industry would benefit the most from manufacturing without the use of dragon scales as a base?

The truth of the matter was that everything made from a scale base could have natural elements taken out and substituted for synthetic ones. The products produced may not be as cheap to the consumer, but would the overall manufacturing costs be lower? The other question burning through her mind was which industry had the biggest profit margin. Chances were the money trail would lead to the source of the dragon attacks. If they didn't prove to be a naturally occurring virus, that is. But Serrah doubted it. She could smell a conspiracy a continent away. And this one smelled like a shit pot full of creds.

A knock at the door interrupted her line of thought.

An inexplicable thrill moved down her spine. Archer had returned with her snack and the files. She didn't know which of the three excited her more—seeing the handsome director again, getting to eat, or reading the physiologist's report.

She opened the door and Archer thrust a basket of fruit and bottled water into her hands. He moved by her and closed the door. With hand still braced against it, he said without preamble, "The reports are missing from both electronic and hard copy files."

Her appetite took another detour as she processed the unlikely words. She set the fruit basket on the bedside table and crossed her arms over her chest. "What else is missing and who has access to those files besides yourself?"

He paced around her room in agitation. "I didn't notice anything, but then I only looked for those particular files. As far as access, I'm the only one—besides my office manager, Mercia. But I don't know why she'd take them. Look, if my staff had asked for them, I would have granted the request. There was nothing in them that needed to stay hidden."

Serrah jumped on that bit of information. "Did someone ask and you've just forgotten?"

"No. I remember putting the hard copies into the cabinet. I never went back in there afterward." He stopped by her comm station and glanced at the screen. "Pharmaceuticals."

"What's that?" She moved to stand beside him as they both looked at the screen.

"The majority of sloughed dragon scales go to manufacture pharmaceuticals."

And what bigger industry was there than that of maintaining health on this and other worlds? "I'll start there."

She turned to him, taking in the bleak expression in his lagoon eyes. "I suggest you contact the physiologist and have him send you another copy of that report. I can wait a few days to read it."

The man struggled with some big issues within his small community. If he hadn't misplaced the files, that meant someone close to him had taken them so he couldn't share them with anyone outside, which meant there had to be something in them that was significant regardless of findings to the contrary. Quite the mystery.

Serrah raised her hand and cupped his cheek in her palm. "I know this is difficult for you, but I'm glad you told me. It means someone's working from the inside and if they're here, I can find them for you. We *can* stop this."

His pupils dilated and he pressed closer to her hand. Only then did Serrah realize how intimately she'd touched him. When she tried to pull her hand away, Archer captured it in his own. "I know. I don't doubt your capability, Agent Gayle. Not for a moment."

She gave him a hesitant smile. "Call me Serrah."

"Then call me Darion."

Warmth rushed from her core to her limbs. She repeated his name in her mind. Silently rolled it around on her tongue, liking the way it tasted.

Whoa. Way off topic. She needed to concentrate on the case and what it meant to all of society should the dragons become extinct. A very real and depressing possibility.

Darion moved closer. His wide, solid chest touched her breasts. Her nipples tightened at the contact. He brushed a thumb at the corner of her eye. "What's wrong?"

"I don't think it's something you'd want to hear."

Those unfathomable eyes of his grew dark with what she thought was desire. "Try me."

"I was only contemplating the ramifications of the dragons' extinction."

He blew out a breath and stepped away from her, breaking the moment. "I live with that worry all day, every day."

She could tell by his body language—the weary set of his broad shoulders, the sorrowful expression, the clenched hands—that working with the dragons wasn't just a career for him, but a labor of love. It was the same with her. Putting criminals behind a prison force-shield was what gave her a reason to wake in the morning.

"I promise you, I won't stop until I find the person or persons responsible for this."

"The dragons are very lucky to have you on their side." A slight smile lifted the corner of his mouth.

She returned it, but then grew stern. "Also know that no matter who took the files from your office, I will go after them without hesitation, regardless of their relationship to you, whether they be father, brother, mother, sister or lover..."

Darion turned back to her and placed a gentle hand on her lips. "I have no one here that's so close to me, but thank you for the warning."

Words stuck in her throat at the penetrating look he gave her. It was as if he believed the harder he gazed into her eyes, the more he could uncover about her. But that was impossible. She'd never been able to communicate telepathically with humans. Only the dragons, and then just enough for one to tell her she was pretty. If she could hear Darion's thoughts, she wondered if they would be the same as that long ago dragon.

But then it didn't matter because her eyes slid shut as his mouth descended on hers. His lips were warm and gentle. His hands cradled her face as delicately as if he held a dragon egg.

The taste of him slammed into her. Her entire chest wanted to expand with emotion. She brushed against him, letting the hard ridge of her nipples touch him, letting him know what she was incapable of saying.

He let out a long moan that filled her mouth, pressing her lips open with his tongue. She met him halfway, sliding hers against the velvety softness of his. Electricity shot through her body, making her gasp. It was like touching her tongue to live current.

With an abrupt motion he pulled back from her, dropping his hands from her face. "I'm sorry. I shouldn't have done that, it was inappropriate of me."

Inappropriate? Her legs were shaking from instep to groin. With very little encouragement she'd pull him to the covered bed and let him get as inappropriate as he wanted with her.

Serrah fell onto the desk chair and held up her hand. "It wasn't as if I tried to stop you. But I think you're right. We need to keep focused here."

"I should go. I still have to try and contact the physiologist and talk to my crew about the search in the morning."

"You don't have to leave." Her gaze raked him up and down, stopping at the sizable bulge he had no chance of hiding behind the soft twill of his drawstring pants.

"If you keep looking at me like that..." He shook his head. "I'll see you sometime tomorrow."

He started for the door.

Damn it. She hated the idea of him climbing all through the mountains looking for a dead dragon and wasting time that could be spent helping her find who inside the settlement worked to destroy such noble creatures.

She swallowed. What she was about to do went against everything she learned growing up. It flew in the face of all her fears. But then, what fears could she have about dragon tamers now? She was a grown woman, not a little child. Not to mention she had an arsenal of weaponry at her disposal. It wasn't as if the dragon tamers were going to come back to the planet *en masse* to spirit her away. It wasn't as if the rumors about them had been in the least true.

"Wait."

Darion turned to look at her. His dark brow rose in question.

"There's an easier way to find out which dragon died."

"How?"

She held up a finger to indicate she needed a minute.

Taking a deep breath, she closed her eyes and imagined the dark blot of the Agate dragon as it stood on the cliff. The rush of awareness made her head spin as it connected with a consciousness so foreign to her own, and yet so deeply familiar.

"Tamer?" A deep voice like music filled her mind.

"No. I'm an IFM agent. My name is Serrah Gayle. I need the name of the dragon whose lament you sang tonight. Director Darion Archer wants to know."

A rumble like laughter filled her, shimmering down into a well she thought long dried. It was the same lovely tone from that day she watched the dragons flying overhead. This dragon had been there. *"I am Arcane and we've waited so long to hear your voice, Serrah Gayle. Tell Darion it is Cedrica who has taken the light path."*

"Thank you."

A gentle brush as if someone stroked her hair moved over her. Serrah took a shuddering breath and opened her eyes.

Darion looked at her with worry. "Are you all right?"

"Fine." She stood and walked on not so steady legs to him. Placing a hand on his arm, she said, "It was Cedrica."

Lagoon eyes widened. His nostrils flared. "You're a tamer."

She shook her head. "I'm an agent."

"One who can speak to the dragons." He wiped a hand down his face. "Do you know what this means?"

Unfortunately she did. She'd just exposed a very dangerous secret to a stranger. "Yes. You have to promise not to tell a soul."

Incredulous laughter tumbled from his mouth. His eyes sparkled. Without warning he picked her up and swung her in a circle. "I knew the moment I saw you in the terminal, you'd be amazing. I just didn't know to what extent."

It wasn't the reaction she'd expected from him. Not by a long shot.

"Put me down!" She hit his shoulders with tight taps. "You should be afraid, not happy."

"Afraid? Why would I be afraid that you're a tamer? It's the best thing to happen to this settlement in over a decade."

Now his reaction really shocked her. "I'm not sure I understand."

Darion set her back on her feet and moved the bed curtain aside so he could sit down. He held onto her hand and pulled her down beside him. "Don't you? Because of you, we can get a firsthand account of what's happening direct from the source. We can ask them where they've gone, what they've eaten, what or who they've been in contact with when they leave the settlement."

Gods, why hadn't she thought of that before? Because she'd been thinking like an agent and not someone who worked with dragons on a daily basis, that's why. Darion knew the pitfalls of maintaining the hatching grounds. Communication had to be a huge obstacle in his job. However, it still wasn't safe to let her ability become common knowledge.

"I must reiterate how important it is for you not to tell a soul."

He frowned. He still held her hand in his. With his other he made lazy circles over the back of hers. "All right."

The need to explain her position welled up. "I wasn't sent here because I'm a tamer. The IFM doesn't even know I can communicate with the dragons. They sent me here because they suspected sabotage. I'm almost sure of it."

His frown deepened. "It's nothing to be ashamed of, Serrah. It's a wonderful ability. Do you know how many times over the years I wished I could hear just one word from them? My job would be so much easier. As it is now, I have to guess what they're trying to tell me. We've worked out a crude system, but sometimes it can be very frustrating."

They sat in silence for a moment. Darion stopped stroking her hand and looked up at her. "Which one did you speak with?"

"Arcane." The thought of what the Agate implied about waiting for her to speak with the dragons ran through her veins like ice water. They had known about her, but kept their silence all these years.

"No wonder he's the one who started the lament. Cedrica was a hatchling in the same season as him. They were very close."

"Cedrica is—was a female?"

"Yes. So was Sorcha, so was Albeana. The blight only seems to affect the females so far. I've been wondering if it's passed on through the mating flight."

It was Serrah's turn to frown. "And your physiologist couldn't answer any of these questions for you?"

"No. He said all his tests came back normal. The only evidence on the dragons was in the visual inspection. Blood samples and swabs all came back normal. He felt it was a bacteria or viral infection, though he found no evidence on the tests to support that."

"I don't believe it for a moment. Even if you cut your finger and get an infection, the swab will grow out something even if the source isn't systemic. From what you described to me on the way here, the entire dragon is eventually affected. And very quickly, too. The only way the slide would come back as normal would be if there was no basis for the infection. One that's unknown."

Darion crossed his arms. "I don't like what you're suggesting."

"Neither do I. Get a copy of the report and I'll call some biologists in from the IFM. Better yet, I'll find out what samples we need to collect and I'll ship them to the IFM lab myself. I'll bet you my last cred that the reports we get back won't match the one your physiologist wrote."

Darion stood. "This is too much to take in tonight." He ran a hand through his dark hair. "Since I already know where Cedrica's cave is, it won't take me long to go there and return."

"If you already know which dragon died, why do you need to go?"

Serrah watch him swallow and the same pained expression filled his eyes that had been there before. "Because I have to burn the remains. It's the only way I know to slow the spread of the blight."

Chapter Seven

A dragon tamer!

Darion still had a hard time believing it.

Serrah had hidden her secret well, but for the fact the lament had torn through her at dinner. It was bad enough knowing the pain the dragons felt at one of their own passing, but to be able to experience that pain as if it happened to her personally—well, there weren't any words. Darion would have given his left arm and first-born son to be able to connect with the great beasts in such a manner.

He, Ontonio and Palmer slugged through the dense foliage that covered the path to Cedrica's cave. His thoughts hadn't strayed far from Serrah since he'd left her hut the night before. The electric shock of their kiss still tingled on the tip of his tongue. It had been like touching a flame. He didn't know what had come over him, or why he'd broken his personal code to take her into his arms and kiss her. Not that she seemed to mind. No, instead she'd opened to him as if she'd wanted nothing more than to know his touch and kiss.

He'd felt the hard peaks of her nipples against his chest and it had almost knocked him off his feet. Heat spiraled up from his groin to his chest, lighting him on fire. He couldn't wait to return to the settlement and see her. During the night, he'd wrestled with the thought that Serrah being sent to Calusia was not an accident. The IFM knew exactly what they were doing. Or had it been a bit of divine intervention? Either way, he didn't intend to squander the time they had together. As long as he kept the chief focus on the dragons and their plight, why would it matter if he made overtures to begin an affair with her? Unprofessional? Maybe, but at the same time something about her called to him. He figured he owed it to both of them to see where their attraction led.

A dragon tamer.

His mind returned to that fact.

Darion never understood why those who had the innate ability to speak telepathically with dragons were called tamers. No one could tame a dragon. The entire idea was ridiculous. Perhaps it grew out of the old circus performers taming wild animals for shows under a tent.

Darion remembered performers back when he was a child who traveled the world with their bonded dragons doing aerial shows. It had been over twenty-five years since the aerial shows had been disbanded and the tamers run off the planet under suspicion of being at the root of a child abduction ring.

The very thought curdled his stomach. Tamers cared more for their dragons than they did the human race. They'd be more likely to steal an egg from a hatching ground to raise that dragon to mate with their own to strengthen bloodlines than they would even care about a human child. Secondly, the dragons would have never condoned such an act.

The stories were rumors. Nasty, ugly rumors without foundation.

The trail opened up to the mouth of a deep cave. Darion lifted the kerchief over his nose and mouth and lit his torch to carry into the putrid darkness. Could this outbreak have been avoided had the dragon tamers remained on planet? It was hard to second guess such a thing, but it didn't stop Darion from wondering.

Cedrica's cave was hidden on the western pass of the mountain chain, not too far from the settlement. She had been a very social dragon and loved to spend her time swimming in the lagoon with her human friends. It was nothing to see her dragging four or five skiers behind her body as she cut through the clear pristine waters.

Knowing he'd never see the spectacle again lay heavy in Darion's chest.

They found the large Topaz on her side in the main chamber. Her once amber-hued scales were tarnished, dull and in some places bubbled up as if burned by acid.

The area around her body held no sign of eggs, or possible hatchlings. Darion specifically remembered seeing Cedrica airborne during the mating flight. She'd been covered by an Opal named Rune.

"Go look in the other chambers for eggs," he directed Ontonio and Palmer. "She had to have hidden them before she died."

They took off deeper into the separate chambers in search of the precious dragon eggs. Each female who died had left behind a small cache of eggs that Darion hoped would hatch and replenish the depleting population. The new hatchlings could never replace those dragons felled by the virus, but with each new lay the chances for saving the species grew—that was if the hatchlings were viable. The possibility remained that the baby dragons would be born deformed or infected.

He tried not to dwell or speculate on the health of the hatchlings. *Don't count your dragons until they hatch.*

When he heard Ontonio and Palmer move away from the central chamber, Darion set his backpack down in the sand

and pulled out the specimen vials he'd taken from the infirmary.

The sterile vials might not be approved by the IFM, but the opportunity to get samples to Serrah and her colleagues was right before him. He'd be a fool not to take it. Who knew when another dragon would succumb to the blight? If they could get answers from Cedrica's corpse they may be able to save others.

He spent time scraping the blight from the scales and collecting tissues from underneath. He wished he had time to cut her open and extract tissue from her organs, but it would be too vast an undertaking in the time allowed. Not to mention the questions he'd have to answer.

Serrah had been very insistent the night before, and she was right. Darion couldn't afford to trust anyone at the moment. Whoever took those files from his office could very well be among his most trusted and beloved friends. He had to be careful.

He'd just finished stowing the last of the vials into his pack when he heard Ontonio and Palmer enter the chamber.

"You were right," Ontonio said, hefting a large gray-speckled egg up to show Darion. "She hid them in a chamber with a hot spring. It's at least a hundred and twenty degrees in there."

Darion looked to the body of the dead dragon. "Clever girl. You knew I'd look for your eggs, didn't you?"

"They were buried in the sand next to the edge of the pool." Palmer placed his egg carefully into his own pack. "There were only three of them."

He'd wished for more. But three was better than the alternative of not finding any. "Three more than we had a few moments ago. Hand me the other one and let's light the fires and go."

Chapter Eight

Serrah hadn't slept well the night before. The bed was comfortable enough, but her thoughts were anything but. Images of dying dragons falling from the sky and urgent voices persuading her to join them kept filling her dreams with terror. She'd woken several times bathed in sweat with her heart racing.

Now in the light of day the nightmares seemed stupid. From what Darion said, the dragons preferred to die alone in caves. She imagined by the time a dragon died, it was probably too sick to take flight.

Serrah hurried through a shower and dressed. Her straight, shoulder-length hair she pulled back away from her face and tied a dark band over it to keep it in place. It didn't look professional, but with the tropical heat on Cambry, she would forgive herself the lapse in a strict adherence to IFM dress codes.

She dressed in the lightest weight clothing she owned and strapped on her stun-rod, badge and handheld, then headed out the door to investigate the settlement. With Darion gone, she'd have to relegate herself to observing the workers as they went about their daily tasks.

She wandered around the settlement as people moved here and there, immersed in their activities. Once or twice she felt the stares of the curious on her, but then looking around she doubted they had very many visitors to this remote village.

Her walk took her past resident housing, the infirmary and dining hall. Behind the buildings stood an open field—pit more like it—filled with sand and surrounded by security locks and force-shields. In the center, grouped together, were dozens of large eggs, buried halfway up in sand.

The hatching ground.

Serrah took the well-worn path to the gates and stood looking out at the future of the dragon species. How many of the eggs had been laid by females dying of the blight? How many would pass on the fatal infection to their offspring?

"I'm sorry, but this area is closed to tourists."

Serrah turned and looked at the young woman who stood behind her with a handheld and stylus in her hand, making notations. She was a good five years or so younger than Serrah and had sleek dark hair that she kept tied back in a severe ponytail. She wore the same loose drawstring pants and gauzy shirt that Darion favored.

Serrah smiled and held up her badge. "I'm Agent Gayle with the IFM. I'm here investigating the recent dragon deaths."

The young woman looked at the badge then back at Serrah. She raised a dark brow. "I heard an agent was coming, but I thought it would be Darion's brother."

Serrah had a hard time not reacting to that bit of news. Darion had a brother who was an IFM agent? Why hadn't he mentioned that before? "I only go where my assignments take me."

"You'll have to wait until Darion returns if you want to see the hatching ground."

“I understand.” Serrah put her badge away and regarded the young woman with a deep curiosity. “I didn’t catch your name.”

“It’s Mercia.” She hit a couple more prompts on her handheld with the stylus.

The office manager who may have knowledge of the missing files. Serrah needed to tread lightly with this one. “Well, Mercia, I’m surprised you didn’t recognize me from the dining hall last evening. I was there with Director Archer.”

Mercia looked up sharply from her work. “I only arrived home this morning. I was on holiday in Benton Pass.”

Serrah knew the place well. She also knew the proprietary look in Mercia’s eyes. She had already called dibs on Darion Archer and hearing that he had escorted Serrah to the dining hall the night before hadn’t set well with the young woman. However, it would be easier to gain information from Darion’s colleague if she pretended friendship rather than rivalry.

“Benton Pass? I’ve been there on assignment. Lovely place. I’ve been meaning to go back as a tourist, but haven’t had the chance.”

Serrah pointed to the eggs. “How long does it take dragon eggs to hatch?”

Mercia narrowed her eyes. “It depends on the breed. Usually four to six weeks for most. Rubies are slightly longer due to their size.”

“And are there any here that are near to hatching?” From the distance, any tell-tale cracks in the eggs were indistinguishable from the normal multi-colored patterns.

“You’ll have to ask Darion. If he feels your questions are warranted, he can answer them himself.”

"Ask me what?" Darion and his assistants walked up behind them. He looked worn and tired, and smelled of smoke and burnt flesh.

"Details on the hatching grounds." Mercia flashed a superior expression in Serrah's direction, as if she were sure Darion wouldn't answer the question. "She wants to know if any of the eggs are near hatching."

He lifted a hand and the force-shield nearest them grew from clear to a nest of wavy lines, to non-existent. "Be careful. The sand is heated from beneath by coils."

They started into the hatching ground followed by Ontonio, Palmer and Mercia. Darion led them to a patch of eggs of deep blue with light purple flecks. "These should be the first to hatch." He pointed a long thick finger to a tiny fissure along the top of the largest egg. "See here? The outer shell will start to crack and peel away first. It helps the baby dragon break through the shell. Unlike birds who have beaks to peck their way out."

"What about the horns? Can't dragons use their horns to poke through the shell?" Serrah crouched down and inspected the fissure.

"They do, but the horns are only tiny bumps now and dragon shells are much thicker than birds' shells." Darion moved down into the sand with her, staring at her over the top of the egg.

It hadn't escaped her notice that he hadn't relieved himself of his backpack before coming to the hatching ground. The trip to Cedrica's cave must have yielded something more than just a dead dragon.

Ontonio and Palmer set their packs down and removed large topaz eggs flecked with gray and placed them in the sand.

Darion turned to watch them before giving Serrah a sly smile. "You want to get the egg out of my pack and put it in the sand?"

She felt her eyes go wide. She'd never touched a dragon egg before. Had never been close enough to one. Unable to speak, she nodded.

Darion turned his back to her, looking over his shoulder with a smile planted firmly on his face. "Don't be shy."

She unlatched the buckles and pulled the egg out. The thick shell was warm to the touch. A small voice buzzed through her essence and Serrah opened her mind to the tiny beast within. The thoughts inside the young mind were barely formed and a bit chaotic, but there was an underlying sense of contentment.

Caressing the egg, she set it down and scooped sand around it as Ontonio and Palmer did with theirs. "Is that it?"

"For now." Darion stood and held out his hand for her. "Let's go back to my office and talk."

Serrah nodded, a little overwhelmed by the experience of placing the egg in the hatching ground, and even more so with the look in Darion's eyes. She placed her hand in his and let him pull her to her feet.

As they walked off the hatching ground he turned to his staff, "We'll be in my office if you need anything."

"Don't mess things up in there. I just had to straighten them again." Mercia called after them. "You need a caretaker."

And Serrah knew who Mercia had in mind.

"Speaking of which, we need to talk later, Mercia."

He left the woman with her dark eyes sparkling with hope. It really wasn't fair of him, but Serrah held her tongue. The man could be a hopeless flirt for all she knew.

Darion kept walking and didn't say anything else until they were closed behind the office door, and in absolute privacy. Then he used his mouth, but not for talking.

Darion backed her up to the wall and covered her mouth with his. Serrah opened her lips, accepting him. Her hands traveled up his arms and rested on his shoulders, pulling him closer so they touched from mouth to groin.

His tongue invaded and retreated, until she could no longer stand it. She sucked him into her, loving him. A moan came from his throat and filled her mouth. His hands rubbed her back then moved around to cup her breasts. Thumbs stroked over her hardening nipples. It was her turn to moan.

And past time to stop the kiss before it got more out of control.

Serrah pushed back some and placed her hand over his lips. "If that's what you call talking, I love your opening gambit."

He gave her a lopsided smile. "I've been waiting to do that all morning."

"You could have come by my hut before you left."

"I'll remember that." He pulled out a chair for her. "Have a seat. There's something I want to show you."

"The mysterious articles in your backpack?" she teased as she sat down and watched him as he took his place behind the desk.

Opening his backpack, he slid a series of clear vials over to her. "I collected these from Cedrica. I thought you could send them to your buddies in the IFM."

"Smart thinking. I'll contact headquarters for a pickup." Serrah crossed her legs and leaned over. "While we're on the subject of headquarters, I find it very curious that you have a brother in the IFM and you didn't think to mention it to me."

Darion blew out a breath and ran a hand through his hair. The chair gave a loud squeak as he leaned back. "I contacted him when the dragons began getting sick and dying. He said he'd take care of it. I thought he meant he'd come home, but I guess he passed on the information to his superiors. It wasn't a secret."

"The IFM doesn't work that way. He should have told you that. Headquarters would never allow him to investigate something happening in his home, or involving a member of his immediate family."

The crooked smile reappeared on his face. "In retrospect, I'm very glad that Tavil's still off-world."

Heat rose to her cheeks and exploded. "So am I, but we need to get working."

"Where would you like to start?"

"You mentioned something about interviewing the dragons. We'll start there. We might be able to narrow down our search if we focus on what they know first." Serrah stood and ran her hands down her pants legs. Energy moved through her in a surge of adrenaline. It happened whenever she was on the right track in an investigation. She'd always thought it was inspiration or intuition. Now, she wondered if it wasn't another form of telepathy.

She shook the vials in her hand. "But first let's put these in my hut and let me contact headquarters."

They crossed the commons and climbed the stairs to her hut. A tingle of awareness swam down her spine. She put her arm out to stop Darion from opening her door and moved him behind her.

Crossing her forefinger over her lips, she shook her head.

In one fluid movement, she pulled the stun-rod from her hip and extended it. She passed the vials back to Darion to hold in case she needed both hands to fight the intruder she thought sure was in her room.

She waved the chit in front of the lock and let the door swing inward.

The room was empty, but it hadn't been for long. Her clothes and equipment were scattered over the floor. The mattress was pulled off the bed and lay on the floor.

"Damn it!" Darion came up behind her and took in the mess.

"You do realize one of your neighbors just violated international law by breaking into my room?"

He let out a long breath and ran his hand through his hair. She'd come to recognize it as a nervous habit. "I know. I'm so sorry."

"I'll need another room. Obviously someone has their own key chit to get in here."

He nodded and leaned down to pick up her comm system from the floor. "I'll put you in the executive building. I thought this would be more private for you."

"Come on. Let's clean up the mess and find another place for me to stay. Then we'll go speak with the dragons."

Chapter Nine

After Darion placed her in quarters across the hall from his and she'd checked her comm system to ensure it still functioned properly and hadn't been tampered with, they trekked up the northeast slope of the cliff, moving closer to the waterfall.

The path was relatively clear of debris. The foliage cut back to make the cliff easily accessible to both man and dragon. Over the snap and rustle of leaves came the unmistakable roar of water as it rushed to the cliff and poured over the falls.

"Arcane?"

"Serrah Gayle, welcome to the perch." A flurry of moving branches heralded the arrival of a massive dragon dark as the deepest shadows of the jungle where it hid from the sun's heat. Large eyes like hematite turned to gaze over Serrah's shoulder at Darion. *"You've brought your mate."*

The words astonished her so much she almost tripped on the uneven ground. If it hadn't been for Darion catching her, she would have fallen flat on her face.

His arm tightened around her waist. His breath warm in her ear. "Don't be afraid. As a tamer they won't hurt you."

"I'm not afraid of them." No, more like afraid of thinking of Darion as her mate. Especially in the context the dragon meant the word.

Darion placed a gentle kiss on her temple and released her.

She moved forward, coming close enough for Arcane to lower his proud head to hover before her face.

Another dragon poked its head from behind the foliage. It was the Emerald from the day before. *"This is the tamer?"* A deep voice rumbled inside her brain.

"It is." Arcane nodded.

"She's very small." The Emerald also noticed Darion, but instead of making comment telepathically, gave a small wuffle of sound.

"Hello, Rhian. Arcane." Darion reached up and rubbed the Emerald's long snout. Tourmaline eyes closed and a vibration not unlike a cat's purr rolled up from the depths of the dragon's chest.

"Your mate is a gentle soul," Arcane told Serrah. *"He will be a good father to your hatchlings."*

She let out a laugh and extended her arm to bathe Arcane in the same attention Rhian enjoyed from Darion. *"You move too fast and assume way too much. I'm only here for this assignment, then I'll be gone. I'm not the director's mate."*

"We'll see." Arcane moved his head to the side, showing Serrah where he wanted rubbed. *"There's a place behind my right forward horn that itches."*

"Here?" She moved her hand to a nubbly spot behind the horn in question. It wasn't as smooth and glossy as the rest of his scales.

"Yes, that's the place." He began a low hum of contentment as she scratched.

Concern for the dragon filled her heart. *"Bend down so I can see the area. I want to make sure you..."*

"It's not the blight, Serrah Gayle. That has only affected our females. It is time for my scales to slough. That is where it starts. Fear not."

Just to make sure, she put pressure on his head to bend his neck so she could get a better look at it. "Darion, come look at his scale."

"Not going to trust a dragon's word?" Arcane teased.

"Of course I do. But you can't see behind your own head. Let Darion look at you."

Darion frowned as he studied the spot behind the dragon's horn. Rhian swung his long neck over to inspect the spot as well. "It's just a bit of flaking. He's getting ready to slough. It's not the blight."

Arcane showed his teeth in an I-told-you-so manner. *"Thank you for your concern."*

"I'm so sorry your females have been dying. I'm not going to stop until I figure out why and how this is happening. Neither is Darion."

"All the dragons know your coming here has changed the tide of our destruction. With you we have hope of fighting the blight."

Serrah wanted to tell him that they shouldn't put so much hope in her. What if her best wasn't good enough in this instance?

"I have some very important questions to ask you and the other dragons. In order to pin down exactly where the blight comes from we, Darion and I, need to know where the dragons have been, what they've been eating and drinking. Have they noticed anything out of the ordinary?"

"I'll ask the others."

Rhian was already moving his massive head to the negative.

It took a few minutes, but Serrah followed the exchange in her head. The act of having so many voices in her brain took its toll. A wave of dizziness rolled through her, upending the world and disorienting her.

Strong hands on her back eased her to sit on a large rock. "What's wrong?"

Just the motion of shaking her head to tell him nothing was wrong made nausea sweep over her. She folded over double and leaned into Darion's chest. His arms came around her, holding steady.

The telepathic channels were too wide open to seal them off, no matter how she tried to concentrate in order to do just that.

"Do you want me to take you back to your room?"

"Just give me a minute. Arcane's conferring with the other dragons about where they've been and what they've seen lately. It's just a little noisy in my head right now."

He moved his hands up her back and began to massage the stiffness from her shoulders. It helped a little, but not much.

"The dragons have not noticed anything unusual this season. All is as it always is."

To relieve the pressure in her head, and include Darion in the conversation she answered out loud. "What about livestock? Have you noticed on your flights if any of the herds have suffered from a similar illness?"

"No. We have been diligent in searching out such things after the blight began."

She stood and once more rubbed Arcane between the eyes, then turned and said goodbye to Rhian in the same manner. "I'll contact you if we find anything."

"We'll be waiting to hear."

Dispirited, Serrah and Darion walked back to the settlement proper, exchanging few words. When they reached their quarters, Serrah hesitated outside her door.

"Why don't you come in and we can discuss what direction we need to go now."

He said nothing but followed her inside and sat down in an armchair in the small sitting area.

As far as accommodations went it beat her previous one hands down, but the circumstances for having been given the room still bothered her. She hadn't contacted headquarters yet. They'd not be pleased with the break-in. Her comm unit hadn't shown any signs of tampering, other than being disassembled and thrown on the floor. As for anyone pulling information on other cases, she couldn't tell.

She sat down at the desk and sent an encoded message to headquarters asking that they pick up the vials for analysis. In a shorter message she let her superiors know her suspicions of the sabotage originating from within the settlement and about the break-in.

They wouldn't pull her off the case. She'd been in worse situations during her career.

Hitting send, she stood and turned to Darion. "I'll need a few things from you. First, I want the names, resumes and employment records of everyone who has access to the dragons and their eggs. Next, walk me through the last few weeks before the blight first appeared."

He sat in the chair with his elbows resting on his knees and his hands linked between his spread legs. Dark circles lined the underneath of his intense eyes. The illness and possible inside involvement began to tell on him, even after only twenty-four hours of Serrah's observation.

He looked up at her. Dark hair fell over his forehead in disarray.

"I don't know what you want me to say. It was business as usual. We were gearing up for the mating season, getting the females ready for the flight."

"Whoa!" Serrah held her hand up to stop him. "What does that mean?"

"Before the mating flight we check the females to make sure they're healthy, and administer their shots."

Serrah sank to the chair across from him. "Shots? To the females? And you didn't think to connect the dots?"

Darion shot upright. "What are you saying?"

"Well, it's more than a little odd that you've administered meds to the females only weeks before the blight began and the females are the only ones affected so far. Seems like a correlation to me."

Pacing the room, he refused to look at her. "Impossible. We give those same meds every time the females come into season. Have been giving them for decades."

"Darion, you have a saboteur in your midst. Don't put it past whoever it is to have changed the meds for a virus."

"No."

The desire to scream in frustration was so great she balled her fists to keep from shouting at him. The connection was so damn clear it shone. "Get me a vial of the med and I'll send it for analysis along with the samples you collected. If it turns up clean, then we cross that off the list as a possible method of contamination and keep investigating. If not..." She put her hands up and spread them. “Then we start tracking who left the settlement around that time, or who received packages, or where exactly the meds came from.”

She rose and walked to where he stood by the far wall with his back to her. His shoulders were tense, posture rigid. She placed a gentle hand between his shoulder blades. “I’m going to start following this thread while we wait for the results. I can’t ignore my gut instincts here. I think it’s probably the best place to start when all our other inquiries have turned up nothing.”

He gave her a short, jerky nod.

“I’m sorry, but my job doesn’t allow me the benefit of dismissing something that might prove a logical thread of investigation.”

Darion turned then and his pain lay stark on his handsome face. “I know. I trust you. I just don’t want to believe that someone I’ve worked side by side with for years could be capable of injecting a disease into the dragons.”

“Let’s cross that river when we come to it. You need to be prepared for the eventuality that it will be someone close to you. Or it could have been an accident in the lab with the manufacture of the meds. Maybe they were contaminated by improper preparation and your people gave those meds just as unwittingly as you.”

Appreciation for her words came in the form of his hand skimming down her face. “But if that was the case the files would still be in my office and you’d be lodged in your hut.”

Serrah smiled sadly at him. “Yes.”

Chapter Ten

Deep emotion swept through Darion. Desire lit small brush fires as it moved from where he touched Serrah's porcelain skin to combust throughout his body. Thinking about making love to her when the dragons' lives hung in the balance was a really bad idea. But he couldn't seem to stop himself.

Losing himself in the sweet heat of her might give him a temporary respite from his problems, but it wouldn't change things. About the only thing he'd accomplish by taking her to bed would be to prove his trust in her. To show he didn't hold her position as an agent against her. Even if she may have to arrest one of his colleagues in the end.

If the proof showed an internal saboteur, then good riddance. Darion wanted to be the one to slap the cuffs on and escort the bastard to Kella City shuttle port.

No, better yet. He needed someone to keep him away from the guilty party. No telling what he'd be capable of. The health and safety of the dragons were in his hands, and deep down the failure to do his job ate at his soul.

Killing innocent dragons. It just didn't make sense.

The wide array of products manufactured by sloughed scales had become the cornerstone for many industries. And what happened when a cornerstone was removed? The building collapsed.

Somehow, the fact Serrah had been sent instead of another agent made the pain of betrayal a little more manageable. Her gorgeous eyes, like the scales of an Amethyst, searched his face as if trying to gauge his thoughts.

A dragon tamer. He still couldn't get over it.

Nor did the feelings of desire for her lessen.

Lowering his mouth to hers, he tasted the conviction of her beliefs. She would protect his feelings only so far, but tamer or not, she was a realist. No matter how much it hurt him, she would make an arrest.

Honesty like that was hard to come by and therefore so precious it made him want to be just as honest with her.

"I want to make love to you," he said against her lips. His palms cradled both her cheeks. Under his hands, she trembled.

"Darion." His name came as barely a breath across his skin.

"You want me, too."

"Yes."

"Then help me forget for just a little while."

Her mouth opened and accepted him in. Sweet passion spurred him to drink more fully from her. Blood pounded in his head and heart. His erection was large and painful. He rolled his hips forward and brushed it against her.

A lovely moan rose from her throat and he swallowed it like water.

Gods, he wanted to see her lying beneath him, writhing in ecstasy. Her legs spread wide, awaiting the thrust that would join them.

He wanted to fly like the dragons. To take her on an updraft and dive to the ground while his seed filled her, her own tight passage contracting around him as she came.

Hard nipples brushed against his chest. Never had he been with a woman with more sensitive breasts. He had to see them, taste them, draw them into his mouth and suckle until she screamed.

Wrapping one arm around her waist, he bent her over, bringing the other hand up to cup her through the soft fabric of her shirt. He lowered his mouth and sucked her through her clothes. Her body went limp.

He bit and licked first one breast then the other. All the while Serrah held his head and made sounds of encouragement. The soft press of her mouth in his hair nearly undid him.

But it wasn't enough. He had to be inside her.

Darion backed her up to the bed and slowly lowered her down.

Leaning over her, he removed the band from her hair and ran his fingers through the glossy strands. Everything about her glowed.

"You're the most beautiful woman I've ever seen." He caressed her full bottom lip with the pad of his thumb.

Her pink tongue grazed across his thumb and pulled it into her mouth. Wildly erotic, she almost drove him over the edge.

The front of her pants gaped a bit, and he slid his hand inside. The soft edge of lace greeted his fingers. Oh, he had to see this. A seasoned IFM agent wearing sexy panties under her clothes. That image needed to be appreciated in all its wonder.

Darion unfastened Serrah's pants and stood. With a quick jerk he had them off of her.

She looked up at him, wearing nothing but her shirt and a scrap of lace between her legs.

"Nice." He smiled with approval. "But they just have to go."

She moved as if to take them off, but he stopped her hand.

"Oh, no you don't. Let me."

He put a finger under the waistband on both hips. Teasing them both, he slid her panties down with slow intent. A triangle of pale blonde hair pointed the way to paradise. When she raised her bottom, the shiny wetness between the delicate pink lips enticed him to further exploration.

He placed a kiss on the hair, rubbing his face back and forth. The delicate musky fragrance of her arousal begged him to taste.

He finished pulling her panties off and threw them to the floor. Her knees came up, and Darion opened them to spread her wide.

Holding her ankle, he moved her leg to rest on his shoulder. He bent to his work, tasting her with a long slide of his tongue over sweet, hot female flesh.

Her back arched off the bed and a long moan dripped from her mouth. Her hand fluttered around his head before sliding into his hair. As he flicked her clit, her hips moved back and forth.

It still wasn't enough for him.

He wanted her mindless. Begging. Out of control.

She opened herself up to him, spreading her legs wider.

Volcanic tightness met him as he pushed two fingers into her. Slowly, he slid them in and out, imitating the motion he planned to do with his cock.

Her hands moved from his hair to his shoulders. Every place their bodies touched, he felt the tell-tale vibrations that moved through her body. Her cries became more desperate, until she convulsed beneath him.

Now, it was time.

He stood and stripped out of his clothes. As she watched him undress, she pulled her shirt over her head and lay back, her legs still spread, waiting for him.

A smile tugged the corner of his mouth. The woman had beautiful breasts. What they lacked in size, they more than made up for in perfection.

Her gaze eased down his body and stopped at his raging erection.

"You're the most beautiful man I've ever seen," she mimicked his earlier words.

"Is that so?"

"Mmmm." She nodded and held her arms out for him.

He didn't refuse.

Sliding into her had to be the single most memorable moment of his life. Each thrust brought him closer to orgasm, but he held back, wanting to stay inside the bliss of her body forever.

Was this how the dragons felt when they pair bonded? Did the compulsive need to cherish and protect their mate flood their systems like molten lava?

He soared.

"Come with me," he pleaded.

Serrah rose up under him, lifting her sex in such a way that offered him no resistance to what he sought.

"Darion." His name was a ragged whisper on her lips as she contracted around him.

He threw back his head and shouted in triumph. A king Ruby claiming his female and declaring her off-limits to all others.

And just as surely she claimed him.

His come jetted into her. A part of him given to her in a moment of sublime ecstasy.

She wrapped her arms around his shoulders, kissing his face and neck. Licking the sweat from his chest.

He rolled to the side, taking his weight from her. Gathering her close, he spoke into her hair. “We’re missing dinner.”

She looked up into his face. “Are you hungry?”

He refrained from saying he’d already eaten, but the thought lingered on his mind like the taste of her on his tongue.

He brushed the sweaty hair from her forehead and placed his lips there. “I’d rather lay here and hold you for a while.”

She settled in next to him, half on his chest. The soft feel of her breasts pressed against his side and the way she fit close to him, made him unable to move if he wanted to. He put his hand in her hair and continued to stroke her.

If this was the way it felt to be with her, he knew giving her up after her assignment ended would be impossible.

A soft hand caressed his chest and moved down his stomach. Blood rushed to his cock, bringing him to instant hardness.

Serrah shifted, wrapping her slender fingers around him.

A few movements over him and he was ready to roll her over and slide into her again. But she obviously had other plans.

Her warm moist tongue started at the base of his cock and rode up to the head.

Gods, she really knew what she was doing.

Lips and tongue worked him into a frenzy. She was in turn gentle and demanding.

Darion lay back and gave himself up to the sensations roaring through him. His hips pistoned up to meet her eager mouth. His eyes closed against the incredible power of her ministrations.

Then her mouth left him and he opened his eyes.

Serrah sat back on her knees, smiling at him.

"What?"

"I think you're a closet hedonist." She placed her hands on either side of his hips and crawled over his body, brushing her breasts over his hardness as she did.

"I just know what feels good, and that definitely felt good." He grabbed one of her hands and pulled her up to cover his body.

Instead of lying out lengthwise over his body, she spread her legs and began to rub her wet core over him.

He took her mouth, trying to impress on her how erotic he found her. Bucking his hips once, twice, he entered her.

The serpentine movements of her body brought him to the very edge. His hands held her hips as he ground up into her. Damn, he wanted to go slow. Wanted to savor every last moment of being inside her, but he couldn't. She drove him completely out of his mind. All he could concentrate on was the heat of her body, the delicate pressure she put on his cock and the look of absolute satisfaction on her face.

"Do you feel that?" Her eyes had a seductive look as they held his gaze.

"Oh, I'm feeling it."

She smiled a vixen's smile. "I don't think you are." She moved in longer, deeper strokes over him.

Much more of Serrah's sweet torture and he'd turn over all his worldly goods to her.

"The dragons are humming," she said.

Did that mean they were inside her head while she made love to him? Pack of voyeurs.

It made him smile anyway.

If the dragons were humming, they were happy about something. And with events being what they were lately, any reason the dragons had to show their joy was a blessing—especially if Darion benefited from it.

"I guess that means they approve."

"Very much." She picked up the pace. Her sex ground into him. Though he tried to hold back and let her drive their lovemaking, he couldn't stop himself from taking control.

He tightened his hands on her and rolled them both over. He pulled out and thrust forward in quick jabs.

Sweat glistened on her skin, making her shine. A drop pooled in the notch at her throat. She arched her neck and gave a long moan as her tight passage contracted around him.

He let restraint slip through his fingers and took his own pleasure.

His arms shook as he leaned over her to place tender kisses on her eyes, forehead, cheeks and lips. "Sleep now."

He didn't have to encourage her to do so. Her eyes were already heavy-lidded. Her breathing deep and even.

For a few minutes after she drifted off into a blissful slumber, he watched her, tracing every detail of her face and storing it in his memory.

After she figured out what had caused the blight and who, she'd be gone. Even as a tamer she still was beholden to the agency that employed her. The IFM didn't just let their field agents walk away. He knew enough about that from the little Tavil had told him over the years.

But as he gazed into her sleeping face, how could he not wish her to stay with him?

No matter, he didn't want to ruin the stolen moment by letting the reality of their situation intrude.

Gathering her close, he rested his head on top of hers and drifted off.

Chapter Eleven

Darion woke with a start.

Something was wrong. Something essential to his peace of mind was missing.

He sat up and looked around.

Not his room. Serrah's.

The memory of how he came to be in her bed sluiced hot and fierce through his body. His cock hardened and tented the bedcovers at his waist.

"Serrah?" he called out, wondering where she'd gone.

She stepped out of the bathroom dressed in her shirt and panties. "Yes?"

The woman had a siren's smile as she walked in a slow glide to the bed. She sat down with her round butt cheeks touching the side of his naked chest. Darion rolled so he could put an arm around her waist.

"Just wondered where you'd gone."

Her amethyst gaze lingered on the obvious bulge in the blanket. "Is that all you were wondering?"

"For now." He ran a hand up and down her back. "I really should get dressed and get us something to eat. On the way back I'll grab the meds you wanted to send off to the IFM lab."

Serrah frowned and ran a hand down his cheek. “I think we’re obligated to look at the meds.”

He pulled her hand around and kissed her fingers. “I agree. It just doesn’t make me feel less guilty.”

“Why should you feel guilty? I sincerely doubt you’re the one who brought the blight to the settlement.”

“Because as the director I’m responsible for everything that goes on here. The saying that ‘shit rolls downhill’ doesn’t necessarily have meaning in my world.”

“And it does great credit to your character, but it doesn’t change the fact that until the blight actually began, you had no way of knowing it was even a possibility. So, don’t beat yourself up because you didn’t stop an attack you never saw coming.”

Darion stared at her a moment, imagining the size of the void she’d create in his life when she left. And to think she’d only been in the camp for a little over twenty-four hours.

The beep of her comm system stopped their conversation.

Serrah kissed him then got off the bed and went to answer the summons.

While she talked in low tones to whoever had contacted her, Darion found his clothes and closed himself in the bathroom, giving her some privacy. Though he wanted very much to hear what she said, he trusted her to keep the dragons’ best interest at heart.

He’d watched the way she’d scratched behind Arcane’s horn. He’d seen the concern in her eyes when she found the beginnings of a slough point on his head. And Arcane had been in heaven having a tamer fawn over him.

It had been so long since the dragons had a human voice to speak to their minds. They must have missed the bonding of such a deep relationship.

Darion started the shower and stepped in. He should have gone back to his quarters to shower, but he hoped Serrah would hear the water running and join him when she finished her conversation.

He was just rinsing the soap off when the door opened. To his disappointment she didn't join him. She leaned against the sink and stared off into space. That wasn't the face of a woman who'd been given good news.

Darion shut off the water and grabbed a towel off the rack and started to dry off. "Well, is it anything you care to share with me, or should I just mind my own business?"

"This is your business." She pushed off from the sink and turned to face him, crossing her arms under her breasts. "They're bringing in another agent."

Darion stood frozen in place.

"I'm not to pack up yet, they said. I'm to continue my line of inquiry until the second agent arrives and then I'll be notified of my next assignment."

When his voice returned and his heart started beating properly again, Darion's rage surfaced. "It's been a day! How can they expect you to solve the case in twenty-four hours?"

"It's not that."

"Then what is it? Explain it to me. No, better yet, I'll contact them myself and request you stay on the case." He shook his head. "I can't believe this."

"I'll take your outrage as a compliment." She turned and headed back out to the bedroom.

He followed her, stepping into his pants as he did. "It's more than that. I trust you. You may have been surprised your assignment on Cambry included dragons, but you jumped into it gung-ho when you found out. The next agent might not do that."

"They will."

"But will they be a tamer?"

Serrah jerked back as if his words were a slap. "I really can't say."

He swore under his breath and pulled on his vest. The fact Serrah was a tamer had little or no bearing on why he wanted her to stay. "I'll be back in a little while."

He picked up his shoes on the way out the door.

Mercia chose that moment to walk down the hallway towards her suite. Her glance moved between him and the closed door at his back. "How's the investigation coming?"

"Slow. Very, very slow." He threw his shoes on the ground and stepped into them. He was as good as caught, and he didn't rightly care. It was none of his staff's business who he chose to sleep with.

"So she'll be with us for a while?"

Gods, he hoped so. "I don't know. We could get a break and she'd be gone tomorrow."

"You didn't seem too interested in seeing her gone when you let her sand the egg today." The words were accusatory. Now, where had that come from?

"Just giving her a crash course in dragon appreciation." Like a tamer needed it, but Mercia didn't need to know Serrah possessed such a skill.

"Does she need it?" Mercia gave a heated look to Serrah's closed door. For some reason it didn't look as if his office manager much cared for the IFM agent.

"No. I'm sure she doesn't. Most people are fascinated by dragons, no matter where they come from."

Mercia's eyes lit as if she had just remembered something important. "Oh, I'm glad you reminded me. My parents are coming to meet you. Isn't that exciting?"

There were no words. Why would her parents want to meet him?

"They're so excited. I told them all about you. Now they can't wait to come."

"If they want to come, that's fine. I doubt I'll have much time to show them around."

"They'll be glad just to meet the man who's taking care of their little girl."

Did her voice just get a little louder as she said that? Was she hoping someone overheard? No, he was just being paranoid.

"Do you think Agent Gayle will be gone by then?"

Darion shook his head. "I really couldn't say. It depends on how long the case lasts. And while we're on the subject, did you move the hard copies of the draconic physiologist's report?"

"No, are they missing?"

"Yes."

"You probably just didn't see them. I'll go look for them."

"I appreciate it." He started away from her. "If you find them, give them directly to me. No one else." He paused for a moment. "Unless it's Agent Gayle. You can give them to her."

He told her goodnight and headed to the dining hall.

With a basket of hot food packed in heat-lock containers, he headed to the infirmary to get a vial or two of the immune boost they used on the pre-mating flight females.

The medication was kept in a locked refrigeration unit and each individual vial had to be electronically logged and signed for. Each entry contained the vial's lot number, vial ID, dragon the drug was administered to and the administering attendant. In this case, Darion would have to log in that the vial in question was being sent to the IFM lab for testing. That way all vials were accounted for.

He unlocked the refrigeration unit and swung the door open.

Empty!

The bin where the drugs were kept was empty. How could that be? They hadn't used the entire lot, and it hadn't been even close to expiration date as to get disposed of. Any leftovers from this lot would be saved to use the next mating cycle. That was the procedure. Everyone knew it.

Darion pulled up the records for the drugs and sat back in his chair as the scope of betrayal began to roll across the screen. The missing vials were all electronically signed out by Director Darion Archer.

Impossible!

He opened the comm unit to Serrah's room.

After a brief pause she came on the line. "Agent Gayle."

"Serrah, I need you in the infirmary. Immediately."

He heard only the buzz of the severed connection.

He locked the office and headed to the front to wait for her. She jogged across the commons, her extended stun-rod in her hand, ready to do battle.

When she reached him, he opened the door and brought her back into the room where the meds were kept. The screen still showed the information he'd found.

"I want you to look at this."

She spent a few minutes reading over the columns. "It looks like you signed out the remaining meds and didn't administer them. Did you send them back to the manufacturer?"

"No. That's just it. They were in the refrigerator and available the last time I checked. We keep all leftovers for the next mating season. There's very little waste when it comes to meds for dragons. They're extremely expensive."

"When was the last time you were in here?"

"When the first dragon, Albeana, got sick I came in to get the antibiotics. Of course I didn't know at the time what we were up against." He ran his hand through his hair in frustration. "The bin could have been empty at that time. I don't know. I wasn't looking specifically for the immune boost."

"All right. And you're sure there were vials left over?"

He pointed to the way the other meds were registered in the log. "If they were used they'd have a dragon's name in this column. These look like they were checked out and wasted. Though even on the rare occasions when we have to waste them, we make a notation in that column to that effect."

"Who else has access to your authorization codes?"

"No one that I know of. If they do, they obtained them without my knowledge."

Serrah blew out a long breath. "Copy the files and I'll send them along to headquarters. It looks to me that someone was covering their tracks. This whole job smells of incompetence."

"Looks pretty competent to me. If killing off the dragons was their main goal, they succeeded."

"Yes, but if they didn't want to make you suspicious they should have left everything in place and you would have continued to believe the blight was a naturally occurring disease." She pointed to the screen. "This is like drawing a map."

"If it's a map, why aren't we getting anywhere?"

"Because we took a detour somewhere." She rubbed the spot between her eyes.

Darion hoped to the gods she didn't refer to their affair as a "detour". He wanted to think of them more as a final destination.

He pushed the thoughts aside and copied the files for her.

"Are your key chits tagged with identifiers on them?"

"Yes. Not that we ever needed them before now. When the tourists started coming here for vacations we switched over to a more secure system."

Serrah leaned over his shoulder and studied the screen. She pointed to the time and date stamp on the entries for the missing vials. "We may be able to find out based on the time the entries were logged into the system and the identifier on the key chit that opened the refrigerator who the most likely suspect is and the one responsible for taking the vials."

"I know I'm going to hate myself for asking this, but why even bother to make an entry? Why didn't they just grab the vials and destroy them?"

"To throw suspicion on you if need be." She shrugged. "I can only guess. Like I said, not the most savvy of criminals I've ever dealt with."

He picked up one of the dinners out of the basket and handed it to her. "Might as well eat while we look through records. It might take a while."

Chapter Twelve

Serrah had the files downloaded to the experts at the IFM. The key chit logs weren't kept on file at the settlement, but were automatically logged into a central computer at the security company that installed the locks. The IFM central office would contact them directly to surrender the logs from the time frame in question.

Circumventing her in such a way wasn't fair—she liked to be involved in every aspect of an investigation—but that was the way the agency worked. What upset her was she wouldn't be able to study the readouts first hand. However, having the logs go between the security company and the central office meant fewer people would have access to the records and less chance of them being tampered with from this point forward.

That didn't mean someone hadn't forged a copy of Darion's key chit. A fact she hadn't shared with him. The poor man had enough on his plate with the conspiratorial evidence already uncovered.

She rubbed her eyes and sat back from the screen.

For hours she'd been going over employment and personal information on those who lived and worked at the settlement. Going back to her original idea when she'd first landed at the shuttle port that everyone was a suspect.

With one major exception: Darion.

Even if the logs came back as his key chit being the one to open the refrigeration unit for the time in question, she would only believe someone had made a duplicate and not that he was guilty of any crime.

Not that she hadn't seen criminals cover their own tracks by implicating all others surrounding them, and plant evidence to point to them as a screen, but that scenario didn't fit this time. In her career she'd seen all kinds of screwy ways people tried to cover their guilt, but not Darion. There wasn't anything in his manner or makeup that even suggested he'd lied to her. No, she could safely say he had told her the truth.

A smile curled her mouth.

He'd been amazing in bed.

Heat unfurled low in her belly.

She rubbed her hands on her legs and leaned forward to look at the screen again. Concentration fled. How was she supposed to get any work done when her mind kept wandering to where he was and what he was doing?

It felt like a schoolgirl crush. All warm fuzzies and dreamy thoughts. She'd never had those feelings before, even when she was a school girl.

Her actions last night had been anything but school girl.

Thank the gods.

He'd brought out her inner vixen. No, better yet, her inner dragon.

They'd definitely performed a mating flight.

And the dragons had loved every minute of it.

While they hummed in her head, Arcane had laughed. He'd known she and Darion were in over their heads from the moment they met.

What would happen when she got her new assignment? She doubted she'd be able to shuttle back and forth to Cambry very often. The island was so remote to any main lands she'd have to take vacation time to see him.

Long distance relationships rarely worked.

She blew out a breath and shook her head to clear it. The file in front of her swam before her eyes. She really needed to take a break, but the work had to get done. Hitting the prompt for the next screen, she settled in to read the dry evidence of someone else's life.

In consideration of the file tampering at Calusia settlement, Serrah worked from a list of employees and used that to surf government servers for employment rather than trust records coming directly from Darion's office. She had so little time left before the next agent arrived she wanted to be the one to break the case before she left. Using files that may lead her on a wild hatchling chase was not an option.

Consulting the list, she typed in the next name.

Mercia Eastmorlyn. The office manager. Serrah did not get good vibes from that young woman. She was protective and suspicious and in love with her boss. If anyone had access to Darion's access codes it would be her.

Nothing threw up a red flag in her employment record other than the fact it was unremarkable. Calusia settlement seemed to be the woman's first job ever. She'd come right from school to work here. Her parents owned a large resort at Benton Pass. So, her family had money. Why would a privileged young woman decide to work at a dragon settlement? After the education records there was nothing more.

Serrah clicked onto the next page and hit sealed documents. Oh, she'd found the mother lode. She filled out the departmental request for more information. Maybe they would authorize, maybe they would deny, but she really wanted to get a look at those records.

Moving on, she typed in the next name.

Ontonio Escabarré, one of Darion's close assistants. His employment record listed an eclectic mix of professions and duties. He didn't look old enough to have so many varied interests, or to have held down so many jobs.

According to the record he'd been at the settlement for four years. His rise to assistant to the director had been a meteoric one, though Serrah didn't see anything that would prove him qualified for such a position.

Then she saw it.

Superior Pharms.

Not farms as in tilling soil and reaping harvests. No, pharms as in pharmaceuticals. She quickly uploaded that page to IFM headquarters and requested a deeper background check. Next she looked up the company in question and sat in stunned disbelief.

Superior Pharms manufactured medicines and products for use in livestock. They also had a large intergalactic division that exported drugs to space ports and other worlds. According to the sales pitch, none of their products used sloughed dragon scales. Their bases were all synthetic. However, they only shared a very small piece of the drug pie.

With that in mind, she did a search for the largest manufacturer of medicines using dragon scales, and the profit margins for both companies weren't even close. Dragon scale medicinals far outsold the alternatives. So, what would be the easiest way to bring consumers over to your camp—kill off the dragons that provided the base for your competitors' products. And how to ensure the dragons became infected with the disease? You place the blight virus in vials of meds that are administered each year to the females. No females. No hatchlings. The dragon population is literally cut off at the reproductive cycle.

She hurriedly typed a report with her theory and sent that off to headquarters as well. They could start an investigation into Superior Pharms from their end, while she dug deeper into Ontonio's background from the settlement.

First she needed to find Darion and warn him of her suspicions. Maybe he'd remember something now that he had a reference point. It was worth a shot anyhow.

After closing out her comm station, she strapped on her stun-rod and headed out to find Darion. He'd said something about working at the hatching grounds this morning.

"If you're looking for your mate, he's in the sand. One of Sorcha's eggs cracked."

"Thank you, Arcane. How is your itch today?"

"In desperate need of a good scratch." The misery was clear, even in his mind voice.

"I'll come to you after I speak with Darion."

An intense feeling that she equated with someone going "on point" flooded her system. *"You've found something."*

"Maybe. A connection I think."

"Tell me!"

The force of the demand made her stagger. She didn't cower from him.

"No. Not until I'm sure. No eavesdropping on my conversation either. And stay out of my mind. You and the others were already there last night at a very private moment."

There was a brief silence then the hum she heard the night before rumbled. *"When a dragon or tamer finds its true mate and they bond through flesh and blood, it is a joyous occasion. We were celebrating."*

What could she say to that? There was no comeback she could make that didn't sound as if she denied the deep bond she felt with Darion.

She closed the telepathic link to Arcane and took the path back to the hatching ground. Through the force-shield she could see Darion bent over an egg. Ontonio and Palmer were with him. Mercia hovered nearby. Her gaze fastened to Darion though he wasn't paying her any attention. His concentration stayed focused on the egg, shaking before him.

A piece of shell broke off and fell to the ground.

A small dark nose poked through the opening.

"Come on, little fella," she encouraged as the tiny dragon struggled to pull himself out of the shell.

"Hard."

"Keep pushing with your nose. You're almost there."

Two little forefeet came over the edge and the hatchling wiggled until he fit through the opening.

"Why doesn't Darion help him?"

Arcane touched her mind. *"Dragons must gain their independence early. As he hatches, he learns problem-solving skills. It is the first lesson."*

Did a dragon just mention problem-solving skills? He sounded more like a corporate executive than a creature of lore.

The shell tipped over and the baby dragon waddled out and shook himself from head to tail. The look of pride on Darion's face stole Serrah's breath.

"Hello." Darion ran his large hand over the tiny dragon's body. "Are you hungry?"

A small crooning noise came from its throat.

"Here." He handed the small dragon what looked like a bite-sized piece of meat.

"Should he do that? What about his mother teaching him to hunt?"

"Sorcha was his dame. She has taken the light path. I will teach him to hunt when he is ready."

The dragon used his talons to climb up onto Darion's thighs. For the first time Serrah noticed the men were all wearing thick leather pants instead of their normal lightweight drawstring trousers. She supposed they did so for the very reason she witnessed now. Having a dragon climb your leg without a protective barrier would be very painful.

Darion looked up then and smiled. He motioned for Mercia to let Serrah into the hatching ground.

"What do you think?" He held up the little Amethyst for her to see.

"I think he's amazing." When she reached him, she put her hand out and ran it over the shiny scales.

"Yes, he is." He scratched the dragon behind the horn nubs, and the jewel eyes closed in rapture.

Love shone from Darion like a golden halo. The man loved the dragons with a protectiveness she'd never seen before. A brief vision flitted through her mind. Arcane was right, he'd be a good father.

A lump formed in her throat.

"What are you going to name him?" She tried to make her voice sound as normal as possible.

He held the dragon up facing her. Its gaze stared into hers as if waiting for something to happen. Darion gave a lopsided kind of smile. "You name him."

"Me? I don't know anything about naming dragons."

The soft rumble of dragon laughter filled her mind.

"Come on, I'm taking him to the infirmary to check him out. You can think about a name as we walk."

She didn't want to leave Ontonio in the hatching ground without first explaining the possible danger to Darion. And yet, telling him now would be very risky. Not that she suspected violence, but why take chances? If the thought of killing dragons came easy, humans probably didn't rank much higher.

Reluctantly, she followed Darion from the hatching ground and to the infirmary. He carried the hatchling to a scale and placed him on it.

"Six point eight kilos. He's a good size."

"He doesn't look that big." Serrah gave the scale a once over, thinking it must need to be recalibrated.

"Dragons have very dense muscles. They look lighter than they are."

"Then how do they manage to fly?"

"Hollow bones." Darion picked up the little dragon again as it started to toddle off the end of the scale.

She nodded. It made sense. They would need heavy muscle mass to become airborne, but light bones to stay aloft, though Serrah didn't pretend to know anything about aerodynamics.

"May I?" At Darion's nod, she took the dragon from him. It stuck its nose in the space between her body and her arm, right under her breast. A long contented purr vibrated his body as he drifted off to sleep.

She continued to rub his head. "Sominose."

Darion smiled. "The Cambrian God of Sleep, a good choice considering." He rubbed the dragon's head and then leaned over and gave Serrah a passionate kiss. "I wanted to do that at the hatching ground."

Her heart beat triple time. “I’m glad you waited. We have a real problem, Darion.”

The heated look in his eyes cooled and he pulled a chair out and offered it to her. “Who is it?”

She sat and waited for him to take a seat as well before she plunged into her findings. “Let me preface this by saying that it’s only a thin connection with plenty of speculations around it, but it’s enough that I’ve informed headquarters to do a full background search.”

“Never mind beating around the bush, you’ve leveled the entire jungle now.” He caressed a hand down her arm. “Just tell me.”

“Did you know that Ontonio used to work for Superior Pharms? The very same company that manufactures the immune boost you gave the females.”

“Son of a bitch.” Darion shot to his feet and started to pace the length of the room.

“I’ll know more when headquarters checks back, but for now you have to watch him. I don’t think he’ll try anything with Palmer around.”

“Unless Palmer is his accomplice.” Darion spoke the very words she had tried not to even think.

“I didn’t see anything in his employment record to suggest he worked for Superior Pharms. But if Ontonio is being paid he could have offered Palmer a lot of creds to help pull it off.” Serrah held up a cautioning hand. “Watch him, but try not to act as if you suspect anything.”

“Now, how am I supposed to do that?” His handsome face twisted in pain. “As soon as I leave here I’m going to want to rip Ontonio’s head off his shoulders with my bare hands.”

Sominose squirmed in her arms and she stroked him until he settled again. "You can't react. There's a remote possibility that what I found is only a coincidence. Do you remember seeing Superior Pharms listed on his employment application?"

Darion shook his head. His lips were pressed into a tight line. "I'll have to go to my office and pull the paperwork."

Mercia walked in. It didn't escape Serrah's notice that the woman hadn't bothered to knock first.

"Sorry to bother you, but another egg has started to crack."

"I'll be right there." He waved a hand in a shooing motion at her.

The look she sent Serrah was nothing short of pure hate. When the door clicked shut behind the young woman, Serrah stood up. "I should leave you to attend your hatchlings. I promised Arcane I'd give him a scratch."

His features softened as he gazed at her. The white line of tension around his lips disappeared. "You've meshed well here."

She let out a crack of disbelieving laughter. "Not if you ask Mercia. She can't wait for me to take the first shuttle out of here."

"What makes you say that?" Darion crossed his arms over his wide chest, waiting for an explanation.

"Because she's in love with you." With that, she turned and started out the door with little Sominose still sleeping in her arms. She stopped before opening it. "There's something in her youth that showed up on my search. Sealed records, so I don't know what it is. It might be nothing. Youthful high jinx gone afoul. Just be careful."

"I will." He hurried over to her and kissed her again before she left.

Gods, she could get used to that.

Chapter Thirteen

Darion felt like hell.

There was a hole the size of the Relic Volcano in his chest. Serrah asked the impossible of him when she instructed him to not react. How was he supposed to keep from it? Everyone would know something was wrong as soon as he hit the hatching ground. Of course, he could always lay the blame on Serrah and the investigation. It was the truth, after all. Just not in the way he'd make it sound.

Mercia fell into step beside him as he entered the grounds.

"She's made you mad. I can tell."

He kept his eyes forward. If he didn't look at her, maybe she'd go away. He didn't need the complication of having one of his staff in love with him, especially when he didn't return her feelings. Everyone knew of his rule against having affairs with coworkers.

"The entire situation makes me mad. The fact I had to call in the IFM makes me mad. Not being able to stop the damn blight makes me mad."

"Is she close to finding out the source?"

"I don't know."

"She didn't tell you?"

Darion stopped and turned to her. “She’s here under the direction of the IFM. She doesn’t have to tell me anything about the progression of her case.”

“So you asked and she refused to tell you?”

“Why are you interrogating me, Mercia? Do you have something you want to confess?” Damn, he shouldn’t have said that. Not with the sealed records in her background.

Color leached from her face. “What do you mean? You think I poisoned the dragons?”

That wasn’t what he meant at all, he was talking about Serrah’s observation, but the fact she’d used the word poison made him narrow his eyes. “Did you?”

She shook her head and tears filled her eyes. “No. How could you even think that? I love the dragons. I love...” The words choked off on a sob and she ran from the hatching ground, kicking up warm sand in her wake.

Palmer made a face and shook his head at Darion. “You’ll probably regret that later.”

“Most likely, but I’m not going to worry about it now. Which egg cracked?”

“It’s one of Cedrica’s.” He pointed to the egg Serrah had buried the day before. “She must have been hiding them for a while in that cave.”

“Let’s just hope this hatchling is as healthy as Sominose appears to be.”

“Who?”

“That’s what Agent Gayle named Sorcha’s hatchling.”

Palmer merely raised his brow. “Did you happen to see Ontonio on your way over?”

A small bubble of alarm began to spread. He struggled to keep his tone neutral. “No. Where’d he go?”

Palmer shrugged and squatted over the sand. “Said he had something to do. I figured he had to take a lav break. But that’s been a few minutes now.”

The egg wobbled and a sizable fissure split the top. This dragon was coming into the world with a vengeance. A pearly nose shone through the crack. It would be an Opal dragon. They were rare, and even rarer if it proved to be a female.

A small kitten-like mew came from inside the cracked shell. The long nose battered the interior as if to say “let me out”.

An angry cry reverberated the shell lining, splitting the sides with sound.

“Has a temper.” Palmer peeked into the crack.

The dragon’s head popped out of the ruptured shell. Eyes the color of pale aquamarines blinked up at Darion. The dragon tilted its head to the side. A disgruntled sound came out of the little mouth.

“You’ve got to get yourself out of this mess. I can’t help you. When you get out, I’ll pick you up.”

It hissed at him as if not liking his answer in the least.

Palmer laughed. “I’ve known women like that. Mew and bat their eyes, but when they don’t get what they want they turn on you.”

The dragon withdrew into the shell again then came at the opening with enough force to bust out. Triumphant, it stopped and let out a sizable trumpet for one so small.

“Come here.”

It waddled over to Darion. He picked up the hatchling and checked under the tail. A smile hitched up the corner of his mouth. “It’s a girl.”

Palmer slapped Darion on the back. “An Opal female. Doesn’t that just beat all?”

Yes, it did. And judging from Palmer's reaction he had no part in killing the dragons. If he did, he was an unwitting accomplice just like Darion.

"Hey, what's wrong? You should be celebrating. Her first slough is going to set the settlement up pretty for years." Palmer put a hand on the Opal's head and rubbed her behind the eye ridge. It was said that the first slough of a female Opal made powerful aphrodisiacs.

Darion didn't like the length of time Ontonio stayed away from the hatching ground, especially when Serrah was out there alone with a hatchling. "I'm going to go weigh her in and check her out. Contact me if Ontonio doesn't return in a reasonable amount of time."

"What are you considering reasonable?"

Darion didn't answer. He left the grounds before he ended up telling Palmer to watch Ontonio's movements.

The rare dragonette weighed in at a little over four kilos. Much smaller than the male born from Sorcha's cache.

"Let's go find Serrah and introduce you to Arcane."

As he locked the door behind him, the Agate dragon in question let out a ferocious trumpet. Anger filled the skies as dragons bellowed and screamed. They circled overhead, sweeping in from the upper mountain peaks as if readying for an aerial assault. This reaction wasn't from a dragon death. No, this crime tore at their very soul.

Oh, gods!

Serrah!

Chapter Fourteen

Arcane bent his head down, nuzzling her neck. It tickled like a cold, wet breeze.

"Will you stay on after your assignment, Serrah Gayle?"

"If I do, I'll have to quit my job, leave the IFM. I like it there. I feel like I make a real difference in the world."

"You would make a difference here." He turned his head so she could reach a spot lower on his neck. More signs of slough.

"You're only saying that because you can tell me directly where you want scratched. I don't have to guess."

"Come back here, hatchling." Arcane's tone was patient, but firm with the little one as it frolicked in the thick grass between rocks. *"Stay close. There may be danger."*

Sominose stopped playing and tried to hunker down behind a rock as if to hide.

"Shame on you, Arcane, you're frightening him."

"Better he be frightened now, than dead later."

Well, she couldn't very well argue with that.

Leaves behind her rustled. Pain exploded in her shoulder, tearing muscle and flesh. An arrow stuck out of her, buried up to the fletching. She dropped to her knees in agony.

Arcane let out a deafening roar of anger and turned on Serrah's attacker. Whoever had shot her had already taken off through the thick jungle away from the scene of the crime. In less than a second she had her stun-rod extended and in her hand, charged to max.

She started to stand and go after her assailant, but Arcane placed a forefoot in the center of her chest and pushed her onto the ground. Her stun-rod fell to the rocks and rolled away.

"Let me up."

"You'll not hunt your attacker in this condition."

"He'll get away."

"And you'll injure yourself further."

Air refused to come into her lungs. The arrow had most likely pierced her lung as it entered. Energy fled and common sense prevailed. If she was dead, she'd never bring criminals to justice again.

"Can you take me back to the settlement?"

"Sominose, come. The tamer is hurt."

The little dragon came out of his hiding place, scampering on short chubby legs to her. She scooped him up with her good arm, barely able to hold onto his smooth tender scales.

Arcane lifted a forefoot and curled it around her body. *"Hold still, Serrah Gayle. I will try not to hurt you."*

"I trust you. Just get me back to Darion."

The great beast leapt into the sky, taking on height. She tried not to think about the ground getting smaller beneath her, or that there was nothing between her and certain death should she fall.

The skies around them were filled with angry dragons, all screaming in outrage. Rhian rode close to Arcane's wing, his eyes glittering with vengeance.

"Did you see who did this to our tamer?"

"No sight. Smelled." Arcane's admission startled Serrah. If Arcane had smelled the assailant and let him or her so close then it was someone well-known to the dragons. Someone they trusted.

"Who was it?" Her question went unanswered as they landed in the commons.

Arcane lay her on the ground, then moved to the side to give the workers room.

Darion loomed over her, backlit by the midday sun. "It's all right, Serrah. We'll get you to the infirmary."

Mind speech was much easier than verbal at the moment. Talking took too much energy, and breath. She had neither left.

"Stay with me, sweetheart. Please." He put his arms under her legs and back and lifted her.

"Darion, she needs to go into the city. We don't have the facilities to treat her injuries here." Palmer stepped forward to block Darion's way.

"We don't have time to wait for a medic pick-up."

Serrah followed the conversation, but wished she hadn't. She must look like death resurrected. Palmer shifted his gaze from her shoulder wound to Darion's determined expression.

"Let the dragons take her. I don't think they'll complain." Palmer rubbed a hand down Rhian's side as if trying to gain permission for what he proposed. "Let Arcane carry Agent Gayle, and you ride Rhian. It will take only a few minutes to get to the city that way."

The dragons were already lowering themselves to the ground for the humans to climb on, the decision firmly taken out of Darion's hands.

"Leave Sominose with Palmer." Darion lifted the little Amethyst from her arms. Sominose let out a trumpet of protest.

"I think it may be easier if we both ride Arcane. I can hold onto her that way and keep her from falling."

"No, let Arcane carry her the way he did to the settlement. He'll be able to maneuver better if he's not trying to steady the weight of two humans on his back."

"Take me to the city, Arcane. Tell Rhian to follow with Darion."

Arcane nudged Darion, trying to get him to put Serrah down so the dragon could once again place her in the massive talons.

"Is that what you want?"

Arcane nodded, and gently curled his talons around Serrah's waist as they took off for the city.

As they climbed higher and the air grew thinner, Serrah closed her eyes to conserve energy. Her mind, however, worked overtime. Who could have gotten close enough to her and the dragons to take a shot? Arcane had been mentioning danger right before the shot. Did he believe the danger only to the hatchling?

Dizziness overtook her.

She no longer knew which way was up and what was down.

A jolt forced her eyes open. But they closed again.

They'd landed in the city. Distant shouts and the sound of running feet flooded her hearing, but she didn't bother to look. Darion was beside her, she felt his tender touch on her face.

She heard medical terms bandied about and felt more hands touching her. Then they were moving. Each bounce of the gurney sent fresh jolts of pain rocketing through her shoulder. Once or twice she heard the distant cries of her own voice. Everything seemed so surreal and disjointed.

It hadn't been the first time she'd been injured on assignment, but it was definitely the most severe to date. She'd broken an ankle once while chasing a suspect through a garbage-strewn alley. She'd fallen off scaffolding and wrenched her back. She'd even been temporarily out of commission after being hit with her own stun-rod on her first assignment—a typical rookie mistake, but she'd never been shot.

Anger swelled like blood from the wound. Obviously, she'd gotten way too close to finding the source of the blight. Had Ontonio placed surveillance in her room? Or had he stuck tiny sensors into her clothing when he'd broken into her room?

She should have checked. The break-in had seemed more like someone looking for hard information, not planting sensors on someone. If that were the case, why toss the room?

Bright lights filtered through her closed lids.

"Agent Gayle, can you hear me?" A firm female voice came from somewhere on her left.

Serrah thought she nodded, but didn't know for sure.

"Squeeze my hand if you can hear me."

She tried to squeeze the hand wrapped around her own.

"She's not responding. Let's get her on life support and prep her for surgery."

Life support? Surgery?

She wasn't that sick. All they needed to do was to take the damn arrow out of her shoulder and reinflate her lung. Easy enough, right?

A feeling Serrah had spent her entire life forgetting began to surface but this time it had nothing to do with dragons or being carried off by tamers.

"Do not be afraid, Serrah Gayle. The dragons will be with you."

"Thank you, Arcane. I'll hold on to your voice the best I can."

Chapter Fifteen

Darion paced the halls and waiting room of Kella City Hospital. It had been hours since he'd handed Serrah's care over to the medical staff. He hadn't taken time to contact the settlement yet. When he'd sent Arcane and Rhian back, he'd entrusted them with watching over the people in his care. He had no doubt the dragons would kill the one responsible for Serrah's injury if they could find him.

Darion had no doubt it was Ontonio. Serrah had gotten way too close and somehow Ontonio found out.

Footsteps behind him broke the quietness of the room. "Darion?"

He turned around at the sound of a familiar and beloved voice. "What are you doing here?"

"Not happy to see me, little brother?" Tavil Archer was dressed in a non-descript manner. The badge and stun-rod at his hip were barely hidden by a long tailored jacket. Eyes the same blue as Darion's were like lasers shooting out of a tanned face. His gaze missed nothing. "I was sent to replace Agent Gayle."

Darion managed to hide his shock by sheer force of will. He'd have his brother back, but lose his lover in the process. "She's still in surgery."

"I'm so sorry." Tavil came farther into the room and stood near the window that overlooked the shuttle port in the distance. "Gayle's a good agent. Very sharp."

"Why send you?"

"I've been working on the case from the other end..." He paused for a moment. "That's not entirely true. I didn't realize it was the same case until headquarters forwarded me the information Gayle managed to uncover this morning. I took the next transport out."

"Then you weren't off planet?" The fact his brother had to lie to him about his former location didn't set well with Darion.

"No. I was undercover, so I had to reroute my communications to you, and make it seem as if I were somewhere else."

Darion nodded, looking directly at his brother. "I'm glad you're home, even if it is in an official manner. When I contacted you about the blight, I had hoped they'd send you."

"And now?"

Darion started to answer that he'd fallen in love with Serrah. That he didn't want to imagine life without her, but at that moment the surgeon, a tall woman with a steel gray hair buzz cut and elegant features, entered the room still dressed in scrubs.

"Mr. Archer? I'm Dr. Marina. Agent Gayle pulled through the surgery beautifully. We've had to reinflate her lung and she's very weak at the moment, but she'll be fine."

Darion let out the breath he'd been holding. He ran a shaky hand through his hair. "Can I see her?"

"Only for a few minutes. If you'll follow me, I'll take you to her."

"When you get back, little brother, we need to have a long talk."

Oh, Darion didn't doubt that a bit. There were quite a few questions he wanted to ask his brother as well.

He followed the doctor through doors marked "No Admittance" and into a large room where gurneys flanked a center station from where health care personnel monitored their patients' vital signs.

Serrah's bed was at the back of the room. Wires and tubes came out of every orifice, real and manmade. Her pale skin looked ghostly against the stark white bed linens.

Emotion was a bitter pill in his throat.

"We're only leaving the tube in her throat until she wakes up a little more. There was significant blood loss, but we managed to stop that and repair the shoulder."

Darion swallowed, though he didn't know how he managed to around the lump. A unit of blood hung from a pole. Tubing stuck via a catheter into her hand, delivering fluids.

He brushed her hair back from her forehead. Gods, her skin was freezing.

He pulled the blanket up higher on her.

The doctor rolled a chair over to him. "You can sit for a few minutes."

He did as suggested before his feet went out from under him. When the doctor left, Darion picked up Serrah's hand and pressed his lips to it. No one so close to him had ever been in this situation before. He didn't know what to do or feel. Let alone what to say to her.

He started with the truth.

"We've not known each other long—only a few days, but I can tell you that I don't want you to leave me."

Was it just his imagination or did her hand tighten in his?

"I think I'm falling in love with you. And I want a chance to find out."

Her fingers definitely moved that time. They tried to squeeze his, but managed only to curl around his own.

Placing a final kiss on her hand, he stood and thanked the doctor for letting him see Serrah, then found his way back to the waiting room.

Tavil was using his handheld when Darion walked in.

"How is she?"

"I couldn't tell. There are so many wires and tubes it looks like she's lost in some kind of plastic jungle."

"She's in excellent hands. This is a first-rate facility."

Darion didn't doubt that for a minute. The staff had taken charge from the time Arcane landed with Serrah clutched in his forefoot.

"What did you want to discuss?"

Tavil shook his head. "Not here. I have a room nearby. We can go there."

"Then it can wait. I'm not leaving the hospital without Serrah."

A strange smile pulled Tavil's mouth up at the corner. "Congratulations."

"It's too early for that. She's already told me she's leaving after this assignment. I can hope she's changed her mind."

"And the fact she's a tamer?" Tavil raised his brow as he posed the question.

"How did you know that?"

"It's why she was sent."

Darion moved to the window and looked out. Lights were coming on all over the city as the sun sunk low behind the watery horizon. "She made me promise not to tell anyone. That the IFM didn't even know."

"Oh, they know all right." Tavil moved closer and lowered his voice. "Tamers weren't sent off world for punishment, they were sent away for protection. The tide of public opinion was so decidedly against them it was felt safer to relocate them."

"And living in obscurity, away from the dragons." Darion crossed his arms over his chest. "You're wrong, Tav, that *was* a punishment."

The brothers stared at each other for a moment in silence.

Tavil looked away first. "Since it looks like we'll be here all night, I'll go find us something to eat."

"You don't have to stay."

Tavil placed his hand on Darion's shoulder and squeezed. "Yes, I do."

Chapter Sixteen

Serrah woke to a fuzzy world. It felt as if she wore someone else's head, and it was two sizes too big. Someone had exchanged her throat for razor blades. Whenever she swallowed her eyes would water with pain.

Her shoulder had been immobilized and her arm lay propped up on a pillow.

A man stood in the corner of her room, looking out the dark window. He looked like Darion, but the hair was all wrong. So were the clothes. Darion would never dress in proper clothes.

"Who are you?" Serrah's voice sounded foreign to her ears. It was scratchy and raw.

He turned around and she knew without the introduction he was Darion's brother. "I'm Agent Tavil Archer. Darion's brother."

"Where is he?"

"He went to get something to drink. I told him I'd sit with you until he returned." He sat down in the chair by her bedside. His badge and stun-rod were on his hip. Either he was visiting in an official manner or he'd not taken time to secure accommodations before coming to the hospital.

He reached into the deep pocket of a dark jacket lying over the arm of the chair. "I'm glad we'll have a chance to talk before Darion returns."

"About the case?"

He nodded. "I've been investigating Superior Pharms for the past year after some irregularities in their shipping methods were forwarded to headquarters. Also, complaints of something resembling the blight in certain contained bovine populations."

"Contained bovine populations? Do you mean isolated farms?"

Tavil shook his head. "Your instincts in this were right on the bull's eye. Superior Pharms tested their blight inside the facility compound, inside the laboratory before ever letting the virus out to the dragon population."

"My gods." Serrah put her hand to her mouth. "So someone working there complained to the IFM."

He gave her a solemn nod. "We knew what was going on, but we didn't know what they were planning to do with the virus. Where it would be used. When Darion contacted me and described the dragon's condition, we knew we had to move fast on this case."

"So, I was sent into the field without being told what I'd face until I got here. Not very time efficient." She raised a brow and then smiled when Darion walked in the door carrying two steaming mugs.

"I thought I heard voices." He handed one of the mugs to Tavil then bent to give her a kiss. When he would have placed it on her forehead, she moved and let him have her lips. He smiled at her and straightened. "Hello, beautiful."

Tavil had an odd look on his face as he watched the exchange: part pride, part envy. Serrah decided that meant

Tavil was probably single and devoted to both his brother and his job.

"I'll leave you two alone. We'll talk later, Agent Gayle. When you're feeling a little better." He stood and put his hand on Darion's back, as he slid the other into his pocket. "Here's the other key chit to my room. I'm staying at the Hidden Lagoon. When you want to come and get some sleep and a shower, just feel free."

Darion took the chit and gave his brother a hug. "Thanks, I will."

Serrah held up her hand. "Darion, go with him. Get some rest. You have to be exhausted."

"You trying to get rid of me?"

"No. Looking out for you. Totally different concept." She gave him a weak smile and her eyes started to drift closed again.

He kissed her again, whispering against her skin. "I like that."

When they had gone, Serrah opened the link that connected her to the dragons. "Arcane?"

"I'm here, Serrah Gayle."

"What's happening at the settlement? Do you know?"

A long mental pause had her worried. Even more so when he said, *"There are two people missing. We have parties out looking for them."*

"Who's missing?" Ontonio most likely. He knew they would be after him. Did he take a hostage with him?

"Your assailant and another person."

"You have to find them before anyone else gets hurt."

"We have no reason to believe they were together."

"What do you mean?" Why would two people leave the settlement at such a time if they weren't together? Did someone follow Ontonio when he ran?

"I'll not explain it to you now."

"Why not? I have a right to know who shot me."

"In good time. It is a matter of the dragons' honor to flush out those who would harm our tamers."

"At least tell me so I can alert Darion and Tavil who to look for." Frustration rode like a current through her veins. She had no idea how to convince a dragon to do something against his code of honor.

"We will sound an alarm for the director and his brother." Arcane's mind voice became a gentle caress. *"Concentrate on healing, Serrah Gayle and come home to us."*

"Damn stubborn dragon."

"Sominose misses you."

At the thought of the little dragon her heart broke. He was too young to understand that she had to stay in the hospital. The memory of his chubby scaled body snuggled close to hers filled her with such sweetness she'd do anything to get back to the settlement and make Ontonio pay dearly for daring to harm such noble creatures.

She looked around the room. What was she waiting for? No one was keeping her against her will.

She started to sit up. Pain shot through the left side of her body. Something in her chest pulled and hurt. Her upper chest and left shoulder were built up like she wore athletic padding. The nurse call button sat near her right hand. She pushed the button and waited for a voice to ask what she needed.

"To get the hell out of here. I don't have time to spare."

No answer came. Instead a young woman who looked no more than a teenager came into the room and pushed a button on one of the many drips going into Serrah's good arm. Knowing the nurse probably just bolused her with mind-numbing pain meds, Serrah brought her hand up to her mouth and pulled the IV out with her teeth.

"Agent Gayle!"

"Get the doctor. I want out of here, now! There are lives at stake."

The young nurse didn't seem to know what to do. "Where did your friends go? Isn't one an agent?"

"I said: Let. Me. Out. Of. Here." Blood dripped from the back of Serrah's hand and splashed on the floor where she held the nurse's arm. "What's so hard to understand about that?"

"You're in no condition to go anywhere."

"ARCANE!"

"Be good and do what they tell you. We can handle the search from here."

"You don't understand..."

"I do. Of all your loved ones, it is the dragons who understand the most. Second only to your mate, of course."

She lay back against the bed, deflated by Arcane's words. *"Darion's a good man."*

"He's the best of men. He and his brother. Trust them to be your legs now. The dragons will be your eyes and thoughts."

"I'll have to stick you again since you pulled out your IV." The nurse took Serrah's arm and inspected her veins, then stuck a bandage on the site that continued to seep a bit.

"No more IV's."

"When your pain meds start to wear off you'll want an IV."

"No. They dull the mind too much. If I have to stay here, I want to have a clear head."

The nurse shook her head. "There is such a thing as being out of your head with pain, but I'll leave it for now. If you change your mind, or the pain gets too much, let me know." She pulled the covers up on Serrah and fussed around the bed for a moment, making her comfortable.

"I have to say, Agent Gayle, you're one tough lady."

"Thanks. Agents have to be or we don't survive."

The nurse left the room, turning off the light before she did.

As her eyelids grew heavier, Serrah's thoughts drifted back to Darion and Tavil. What would they do without her? How would they coordinate their efforts with the dragons without a tamer to talk to them?

"Arcane?"

"I'm here."

"Watch over Darion and Tavil for me."

"Always, Serrah Gayle. Always."

Chapter Seventeen

Showered and wearing his brother's clothes, Darion sat on the edge of the bed and tried to get through to the settlement. So far no one answered the comm system. That wasn't a good sign.

Where was everyone? It was way past meal time so they weren't in the dining hall.

The summons was finally answered.

Palmer came on the line, winded. "Calusia settlement administration."

"It's Darion. Where the hell is everyone? I've been trying to get in contact with you for over an hour."

"We have a little bit of a situation here."

Darion tried to tamp down the panic. "What kind of situation?"

"Ontonio and Mercia are both missing. We've been looking everywhere for them, and the dragons have been searching from the skies, but they've just disappeared. Vanished."

He understood Ontonio, but Mercia. Did she leave because he'd been harsh with her that morning? Was she just off on a sulk and didn't know the entire settlement had been thrust into chaos by the shooting of an IFM agent? Or were there more sinister forces at work? Were they wrong about Ontonio and it had been Mercia who sabotaged the dragons? She did travel back and forth a lot between Calusia and Benton Pass.

"Are the dragons searching the caves?"

"Already on it." He paused then asked, "How's Agent Gayle?"

"It was pretty bad, but she'll be fine. She's resting now."

"Anything else? Suggestions?"

"No. I'm sure you're doing everything I would. I'll try and be back there sometime tomorrow."

They released the connection and Darion leaned back on the bed, resting his hands behind his head. He needed to be doing something productive. It wasn't like him to sit idly by while others did his job. As the director he should be at the settlement. But Serrah needed him, too. She'd been injured while in his camp. By one of his people.

A dragon trumpeted outside, coming from the lagoon. Darion jumped off the bed and ran to the sliding balcony doors. Tavil picked up his stun-rod and met Darion there.

"That sounded like a warning." Tavil tried to look through the crack in the blinds without moving them. "I can see the dragon on the beach, but nothing else out there."

"He's guarding us then, and there's danger coming from somewhere. We should go out and find it, before it finds us holed up in here with nowhere to go."

Tavil gave him the same mischievous grin he had when they were children and about to do something they'd been warned not to. "I was just thinking the same thing."

Making no sound, Tavil opened the sliding door on its casters and moved out onto the balcony. Darion followed him, and pulled the door closed. A short flight of stairs made easy access to the beach.

The dragon trumpeted again. The massive wings flapped and caught the lights from the passing conveyances on the road out front. It was a king Ruby. And he was pissed.

"Darion?" A soft female voice whispered from the bushes beside the door.

Startled, he turned. Tavil shined a light in the intruder's eyes.

Mercia blinked and held her arm up in front of her eyes.

"What are you doing here? Do you know everyone at the settlement is looking for you?" Come to think of it, how did she know where he was and what room he'd be in? He didn't even tell Palmer that he was with Tavil.

The dragon let out another trumpet and started forward off the beach. He shook his head back and forth, trying to warn Darion of something. He really needed Serrah here now. She'd be able to tell what had angered the king Ruby.

"Can we go inside and talk? I'm afraid..."

"Of the dragon? Rubicon won't hurt you." Though judging from the anger in those deep crimson eyes, he couldn't really be sure.

"No, the person who shot Agent Gayle is after me. I saw him following me down the beach."

"You saw the shooter?" Darion grabbed both her arms and looked into her eyes.

"No, I didn't. I saw Agent Gayle get shot. Not the shooter. But I think he thinks I did."

"And so you came down here?"

She nodded. "I was going to go back to my parents and hide. I saw all the dragons circling the city and figured you had to have come here with Agent Gayle."

Something wasn't adding up. But he couldn't put his finger on it. Why take off on her own and make the trip to the city when it would have been safer to just stay at the settlement and seek protection from Palmer and the dragons?

But if the shooter followed her that would explain why Rubicon was trumpeting a warning, but not why the dragon had picked up speed and came even closer to the balcony. Was the man hiding in the thick foliage planted between the suites?

Darion held up his hand at the dragon. "It's all right, Rubicon. Tavil and I will take care of this." He turned to Tavil. "We need to check the bushes. There's a lot of dark crevices for someone to hide."

The dragon roared and two dark streaks flew into view on the beach, answering the king Ruby's cry. They landed on either side and took up the warning call.

"I'll look around. Take Mercia inside before the dragons cause a riot." Tavil walked down to the beach, meeting the dragons halfway. He conferred in low tones to the angry beasts, but Darion couldn't hear what he said.

He ushered Mercia into the room, leaving the door cracked a bit for Tavil. Desperate to clear his lingering confusion about the incident, he continued to dig for information. "Why do you think Serrah's shooter is after you?"

"I was walking on the cliffs, thinking." She shot him a look. A blush rose in her cheeks. "I saw the entire thing."

A violent trumpet and the stamp of the big king Ruby's feet shook the room.

"Darion!" Tavil yelled from outside. "Be careful."

Rubicon screamed again in outrage.

The world spun into blackness.

Chapter Eighteen

A sound awoke her. The moon shone in the window, casting deep shadows across the room. One of the shadows moved, alerted to her awakening by the change in her breathing.

"Who's there?"

Light flooded the room, as she hit the remote on the call bell.

Ontonio stood in the corner by the window, looking at her.

Her breathing hitched, but she tried to remain calm.

"I wanted to explain."

Even from where he stood, Serrah could see him shaking with fear.

She couldn't call for help. If she did Ontonio might panic and possibly kill someone in the process. No, better to let him talk and try to keep him calm while doing so.

"Go ahead."

"I didn't mean to do it." He rubbed his hand around his stubbly jaw. He looked like ten kinds of hell. "I left there when I found out what they were doing."

"Left where? Pretend I don't know what you're talking about." She kept her hand near the call bell just in case she needed some assistance. The nurse could always call security if things got out of hand.

"Superior Pharms. I found out what they were testing and I left. I didn't want any part of it. I didn't know they were going to use it on the dragons—until the blight showed up, but then it was too late."

"Why didn't you tell Darion what you knew when the blight started?"

"I thought he'd blame me. I thought..." He swallowed. "I didn't want to lose my job. It's the best place I've ever been. I love being at the settlement."

"Ontonio, don't you see? You've destroyed records, tampered with evidence we could have used to trace the blight, and broke into my quarters. If you had told Darion the truth from the beginning he could have passed on that information to Tavil and you would have kept your job, and been..."

Her words cut off as the dragons began to roar and swarm the area.

"Arcane? What's happening?"

"It's Darion."

"Oh gods!" She sat up in the bed, the painkillers worn off enough to cause her immeasurable pain. *"Is he all right?"*

"I don't know. I'm going to find out now."

"Ontonio is here. He knew about the blight all along. Did he shoot Darion like he did me before coming here?"

"I doubt it."

"Why?"

"Because Ontonio isn't the one who shot you."

Chapter Nineteen

Darion's vision had shrunk to a pinpoint of light. No! He wasn't going down without a fight. There was no way he'd let some spurned woman take him out while he was too stunned to protect himself.

Forcing his eyes open, he could see a pair of feet directly in front of him.

"You slept with her. How could you do that to me? We were supposed to be together. I told my parents. They're coming to meet you. I told you that."

She might have told her parents, but that didn't make it real. Where had she gotten the idea he thought of her as anything more than a coworker?

The woman was unhinged. Why'd he fail to see it before?

She pulled his head up by his hair to look into his face. "I'll forgive you for fucking that government whore. I'll do anything for you. Don't you know that?"

Darion wished he had enough saliva to spit in her face. But his mouth had turned to cotton when he'd been hit with the stun-rod. He wondered briefly if the stun-rod in question had been Serrah's. She hadn't been wearing it when Arcane brought her back to the settlement after the attack.

"Serrah?" The name fell from the side of his mouth all mangled and slurred.

But she heard and understood. Mercia narrowed her eyes. "I couldn't get a clear shot without hitting Arcane, so I winged her. I wish I'd have nailed her right between her stupid eyes."

Darion heard enough. What a fool he'd been. First Ontonio and now Mercia. He'd always thought he was a solid judge of character. He'd missed the mark by a mile on those two.

Feeling returned to his hand and arm. He doubted he had enough control of his limbs at this point to make a difference, but he had to try.

He stuck his hand out and grabbed her leg. It was just enough to unbalance her. She started to go down, but managed to stay upright.

Mercia kicked at his head and connected with his ear. It already rang from the stun-rod, but it still hurt like hell.

He wrapped his arm around both her legs this time and pulled her down as a crash came through the balcony door and something not unlike lightning split the room in two.

Mercia screamed and fell across Darion.

Voltage traveled from her body to his.

For the second time that night, the darkness called him under.

When he woke again, Tavil bent over him tapping his cheek. "Come on, it's no time to be sleeping."

Darion shook his head to clear it. He swore he could hear his brain rattle as he did. His mouth tasted like burnt lead. His eyes were gritty.

"Did you get the number of the shuttle that hit me?"

"Word to the wise: don't grab hold of someone who's about to get hit with a stun-rod set to max."

Darion, with the help of Tavil, sat up and looked around the room. Mercia lay on her side, long dark hair over her face. Her hands were cuffed behind her back. "Next time warn me you're at my back. Is she going to be all right?"

"Unfortunately." Tavil hefted a pistol-grip bow. There was an arrow cocked and ready. It was the same kind that had been lodged in Serrah's shoulder. "I found this out by the deck."

He just didn't want to wrap his head around it. Even hearing her confess the crime herself, he still had a hard time believing it. Mercia had seemed such a stable, solid girl. He'd relied on her to keep the hatching ground organized. How did she go from being a godsend to the settlement, to their worst nightmare?

Not only had she tried to kill an IFM agent, but she had looked him right in the eyes and lied to him, then hit him with a stun-rod. Probably Serrah's rod. He had no doubt Mercia intended to kill him as well. And over what—because he didn't return her feelings?

Darion tried to stand, but his legs remained rubbery after getting hit with the large dose of current. "I want to check on Serrah. What if Mercia went to the hospital first and that's what set the dragons off? We aren't that far away. If she tracked us here, finding Serrah's hospital room is much easier."

"I have the Kella City Police on their way. After I give a statement, I'll take you over there myself. You're in no condition to be going anywhere alone."

The blinds by the door creaked and Darion knew the night had turned to shit for a second time. The worst part was he had no energy left to fight.

Ontonio stood inside the room looking like twelve miles of rough road with nothing but a bum climb cart for transportation.

He held out his arms, wrists together. "Serrah said to make sure you were all right then turn myself in."

Tavil shook his head. "Wait in line. My cuffs are already in use."

Darion wasn't so forgiving. "Why'd you do it? The dragons depended on you, trusted you...I trusted you and you betrayed all of us."

"I already told Serrah the story. But I swear I didn't know they had sent the blight until it showed up on the first dragon."

"But you knew about it?"

Ontonio hung his head. "I did. I knew Superior Farms manufactured it. I didn't realize they wanted to wipe out the dragons until they started getting sick. They wanted to control the pharmaceutical market with their synthetic drugs. The only way to accomplish their goals was to kill off the dragons, or at least show them as vulnerable. If the source of your product base dies off there isn't much left but the synthetics."

"Then why hide the evidence? Why didn't you just tell me when I went looking for answers?"

"That's what Serrah asked me."

"She's a smart lady." Darion's head pounded. Too much had happened in such a short time. He needed time to process it all. "How did she convince you to come here and turn yourself in?"

"Told me it's not too late to cooperate. That my testimony will help to bring the company down." Sincerity was there in his eyes and voice.

"Well, it's no longer Serrah's case. Any deal you make will have to be through Tavil."

During the conversation, Tavil had been listening but had gone about his business of sitting Mercia up in a chair and trying to bring her around.

Sirens blared in the night, coming closer. Dragons on the beach began to mimic the sound as if taunting the guilty.

"I'll see what I can do," Tavil finally said. "But I can't promise anything. It shows some good faith on your part that you came here on only Agent Gayle's suggestion."

Then the police were at the door and the rest of the night passed in a blur of statements from Tavil and Darion, confessions and apologies from Ontonio and hysterical threats from Mercia.

The mystery of Mercia's sealed record had been solved. In her adolescence, she'd stalked a suitor then threatened him and his girlfriend when he'd spurned Mercia's advances. Only her parents' money and influence had seen her treated in a facility and released. Working in the settlement had been a recommended therapy for her, but the intimate relationships formed with her coworkers and Darion had sent her back into her delusions.

By the time Darion made it to the hospital to check on Serrah the breakfast trays were being handed out to the patients and sunshine shone in the mid-morning sky.

He ran a hand through his hair as he stood in the doorway looking into the room at her. His entire world came down to this moment. Though he knew she had to leave him, every instinct inside him wanted to beg her to stay. But that would make him just as bad as Mercia. She needed to want to stay, but he wouldn't force her or guilt her into it.

She sat up in bed with a cup in her right hand, looking like she hadn't slept much. At least he wasn't the only one worn out.

"I thought you'd try to take a nap before you came back here." She took a sip of her beverage then set the cup back on her tray.

"No. I had to see you as soon as I could. How are you feeling this morning?" He ran a thumb over the dark circles under her eyes. He wanted to remember the feel of her skin in case she left.

"I'm in pain, but very glad you're here. I was so worried when Arcane told me what happened."

He smiled sadly. "So, it seems your case is closed."

"Yes." She turned her face away and stared out the window.

"Any idea what your next assignment will be?" The question got stuck somewhere in his throat and made his voice catch.

She shook her head. "I have to convalesce first. It might be months before I'm ready for another assignment."

Darion wasn't sure how to take that. "Did the doctor tell you there might be permanent damage?"

When she turned her gaze to his, tears stood in her eyes. "No. I'm just wondering how I can leave. Since the assignment began, I've known the case would be solved and I'd move on. But last night, when Arcane told me Ontonio wasn't the one who shot me and that you were in danger...I realized that I no longer knew what I wanted, only that no matter what, I wanted you."

Darion's heart tripped then beat hard against his breast bone. He moved her tray aside and sat down next to her. "You've got me. For as long as you want me."

She smiled and held her palm against his cheek. "Would it put you out if I ask to convalesce at the settlement?"

"I'd have been disappointed if you didn't. So would the dragons, and you really don't want to disappoint them." He kissed her hand then leaned forward and took her mouth.

In that kiss their future was sealed. They would work it out: a relationship with each other and her career. Nothing else mattered, only the life that spread out before them.

The dragons were safe. The blight wiped out.

The next generations secure.

And a dragon tamer to speak with them all.

About the Author

To learn more about Kathleen Scott, please visit http://www.mystickat.com or send an email to Kathleen Scott at mystickat1965@yahoo.com

Look for these titles by *Kathleen Scott*

Coming Soon:

Solarion Heat
The Host: Shadows w/a M.K. Mancos

Hard to Guard

Nina Mamone

Dedication

To Mom—you know why

Chapter One

A wyrm is missing. Check your charges. For those AWOL, meeting at seventeen hundred hours.

Connor McKenna read the message displayed on the pager cupped in his callused palm, his fingers clenching momentarily around the plastic. The pavement under his feet reflected the heat of the May sun up his jean clad legs. The mingling of car exhaust, pollen and blacktop almost eclipsed the aroma of roasted meat and yeast wafting from the hot dog cart parked beside him.

Suppressing a sigh, Connor shoved the beeper deep into his pocket. "Looks like we're up."

Beside him, his best friend Cisco Martin scowled into his own little black box. "That's just super."

Connor's eyebrows rose slightly at his friend's sarcastic tone. Cisco was usually mildly irritable, but he'd been snarking all day.

"What put a burr up your ass?" he asked with mild curiosity. "Chasing after a missing wyrm isn't part of my plans, either, but I'm not getting all tragic about it."

Cisco shrugged irritably. "As if I don't have enough to deal with. In eighteen hours I have to catch a flight to Sedona to find some pampered starlet the adobe hut of her dreams. Preferably where the nexus of psychic energy meets the goddess's pinnacle, or some such bullshit. Agnes wants me to spend a weekend at her house playing Mr. Fix-It and eating charred meatloaf, and since the flue in her chimney won't open I'm gonna have to do it. And now this."

Connor schooled his features. Agnes, Cisco's mother, was a sore spot. Or, more like an open, seeping wound which deserved care. But Connor knew better than to commiserate; sympathy only fed Cisco's sulkiness.

Looking away, he dug in his pocket for change. "You're such a drama queen."

Cisco's eyes narrowed. "A drama *king*, thank you very much. I'm all man. Pass it along."

The vendor stretched out a hand, balancing four hotdogs loaded with chili and slaw. As Connor took the hotdogs, he measured the ache in his stomach and realized the half dozen eggs he'd had for breakfast were long gone. "Hey, give me four more of these, would you?" He turned as Cisco's comment registered. "Pass it along? Since when does Cisco Martin need advertising? How many girlfriends are you juggling now?"

"Two," Cisco said, sneering as he indicated Connor should keep the food with a dismissive wave of his hand. "And I highly recommend it, though I know I'm wasting my breath. How long has it been since you've gotten one woman, much less two? Maybe if you'd put a little more care into your wardrobe, invested in a button-up shirt, for God's sake." Cisco gave Connor a once over, from his shaggy, uncut hair and worn T-shirt, to the hips that usually sported a heavy tool belt and his booted feet. "I don't get it. There's the muscles, the hair. You've got that whole I-work-with-my-hands vibe going on. Women should be lined up."

Connor shrugged. "So I haven't been on any dates lately. I just haven't met anyone I wanted to waste the time on." Though that hadn't been a conscious decision on his part. One day he'd woken up and realized it had been four months since he'd had a date, and even longer since he'd had sex.

Cisco continued to gaze at Connor, fingering his chin. "What about Darla? The blond receptionist, remember? She was into French art house films and lycra? Would you like her?"

Connor choked, swallowed some bun. "No. Hell, no. I do not want, or need, one of your old girlfriends. I can find my own woman."

Nodding, Cisco said, "Right. Anyway, I think I ruined her for anyone else. She could no longer tolerate the lavish excess of bounty that is *moi.* Nearly passed out from pleasure last time we were together, poor thing, eyes rolling back in her head, speaking in tongues. It was awful."

Connor rolled his eyes. The Cisco Show was up and running. Connor knew his friend so well he could predict that, by this time next week, there would be two new, equally gorgeous and shallow women in Cisco's life. Sometimes he had to shake his head at how different they were. But it had been that way since they first met in junior high.

Cisco had had a crappy home life, but was extremely popular with girls and boys alike, a social savant. As an introvert, Connor had stayed to himself, but once he and Cisco had gotten the preliminaries out of the way there'd been no question where his loyalty lay. Cisco brought Connor out of his shell, and Connor wouldn't allow Cisco to shake him loose, no matter how pissy or tragic Cisco became when matters at home got bad.

Grabbing the last of the food, Connor handed two to Cisco. He'd been starving and was down to two himself. He stuffed a hotdog in his mouth.

Cisco held his at arm's length, his thinly handsome face wreathed in revulsion. They were piled high, and some chili slid onto his fingers, like lava flowing from Mt. Vesuvius. Lip curled, he flicked the cinnamon-colored glop onto the grass. "Why do we have to eat this pigswill when there are a dozen perfectly good restaurants within walking distance?"

They were still right beside the vendor's cart. Connor shrugged apologetically at the aproned man three feet away.

"Because I didn't have time for a sit down lunch," Connor replied.

"This isn't the dark ages. Everyone has time for a sit down lunch."

Connor finished the last hot dog, pushing the butt end of the bun into his mouth with a stiff finger. After he'd chewed and swallowed, he said, "It doesn't matter now. If a wyrm's missing, we need to get on it. What are you doing?"

Cisco chucked his lunch into a trash can and walked away.

Connor's eyebrows drew together. "Hey! I would have eaten those!" His gaze snapped to the trash, then the vendor. The guy shook his head and raised his hands as if to say, *not my problem.*

Still walking, Cisco fished his cell from his pocket one-handed and pushed a button with his thumb. Connor followed, scowling.

It was the weekend, but the city was still swollen with traffic. Cars whooshed by, their open windows sprinkling snippets of news and hip-hop. The heavy bass thumps played backup to the sound of distant ringing.

Cisco halted and turned, the phone to his ear. "Connor, I'm saving you from yourself. You don't appreciate it now, but when you're living at the ripe old age of one hundred, I'll expect a thank you note. And a letter of apology."

"An apology? For what?"

"For forcing me to eat cholesterol disguised as fast food."

"I'm not going to waste my time worrying about something that could happen seventy-five years from now. You make it sound like I'm a heart attack waiting to happen."

"Aren't you?"

"No. Look, I don't smoke. I'm climbing on roofs and scaffolding all day. You can't tell me all that hammering and lifting isn't a workout. And I do manage to choke down a few vegetables every once in a while. But, you're right. If I have a choice between dessert and no dessert, I'm going to pick the freaking chocolate cake. If a bus were to hit me this afternoon I'd rather not go to the morgue with an empty stomach. Or worse, with alfalfa sprouts taking up useless space there."

Cisco gave Connor a look that said he was a hopeless case, then turned away to speak into the phone. "Clarice? Is that you?" He paused. "I was worried about you. We've just received some distressing news. It appears one of your brethren has gone missing."

A shriek pierced a three-foot radius around Cisco's head. He jerked the phone away and aimed it away from his ear until the noise died down. Gently touching the receiver to his ear, his calm voice began speaking again, soothing his wyrm charge.

Clarice was a drama queen. You'd think that would be one too many, what with Cisco and all, but the two of them seemed to go together like peas and carrots. Connor couldn't think of another handler who wanted to deal with the constant and needy demands that were Clarice's stock in trade. She was old even for a wyrm, nearly senile. Add to that the nearly limitless avoidance of reality and logic that wyrms were known for, and she was difficult at best, maddening at worst.

Cisco snapped the phone shut and Connor held out his hand. "Let me use that."

"Get your own." But he handed it over.

"No," Connor said calmly. "I leave my Directorate phone at home unless I'm working. Unlike some people, I don't enjoy being available to the whole world every minute of every day."

Cisco shrugged elegantly. "Backward Neanderthal."

Connor waited for Raul to pick up. The first ring came and went, and Connor waited calmly, but by the fifteenth, he was twitchy with concern. "Raul's not answering."

"That's not unusual, is it?"

Connor shook his head. "After the last time, I made him swear he would always carry his phone and answer it no matter what he was doing."

"The irony is almost too much to bear."

Connor stood in the middle of the sidewalk, thinking furiously. Shoving the phone at Cisco, he turned and strode towards the street. He could ride his bike to Raul's, no problem, but the fastest way there was to hail a cab.

"This isn't funny." His gaze cut to the left and right as he looked for an available taxi. "You know how he is. The wyrms are irresponsible children, but with Raul you have an even bigger problem. He thinks the world was designed solely for his pleasure. If he ever had a desire that wasn't immediately gratified, the world would end. He's like a kid in a candy store. Literally. If he was given an unlimited supply of sugar he'd eat himself sick, throw up, then do it all again."

"Surely you're exaggerating."

"I'm not. Though it's not sugar with him, it's liquor. I've seen him pull himself out of a pool of his own vomit and crack the seal on a new bottle."

"Are you going to his apartment?"

"Yeah."

Beside him, Cisco kept pace, his stride long and easy. Of course *he* looked relaxed, his wyrm wasn't wreaking havoc on an unsuspecting city. Connor didn't want to think too much about ramifications, but he'd been a wyrm Guardian for five years and knew how unconcerned the wyrms were for anything other than their own welfare. The trouble Raul could get into made his blood chill.

And it was up to him to make sure that didn't happen. God, he hated this job.

Cisco stopped him with a finger on his arm. "Here, let me try something." He got on his cell.

A minute later, a rare, genuine smile built Connor's hopes. Cisco never grinned like that. He preferred a faintly bored expression, said it made the most of his bone structure.

"Is it someone else?" Connor asked. "Please tell me somebody else lost their wyrm."

Flipping the phone shut, Cisco grinned. "Well, it's a good news, bad news situation. Aw, hell, I can't lie. It's bad news, bad news."

Dread crept up Connor's spine. "Then why the hell are you smiling?"

"I'm sorry. I can't seem to stop."

"Just tell me, dammit!" He clenched his hands into fists so he wouldn't grab Cisco and shake him til his teeth rattled.

"Most everyone's checked in at this point. Only two wyrms are unaccounted for—Raul and..."

Connor felt every muscle he had tense up. "It's Louis, isn't it? He's missing, too. Tell me it's not Louis."

"...Louis."

He slumped, the breath knocked out of him. "Fuck me."

"And you know what that means. If Raul's not at his apartment you have a meeting to attend. A very small, very intimate meeting." Above the divots in his cheeks, Cisco's eyes gleamed. "Just the Director, you...and Sorcha."

Connor's internal temperature shot up twenty degrees and his vision wavered.

Sorcha.

Just the mention of her name sent blood rushing to his groin.

"I *really* need to quit this fucking job," he muttered.

This was bad. The Director's office was the size of a postage stamp. Sorcha would sit mere inches away, delicious smells swirling around her like a cloud permeating the room, causing reactions in his body that were entirely spontaneous. When Sorcha was around he had absolutely no control.

A straining erection pressed against the zipper of his jeans. Jesus. All he had to do was think of her and he was in full rut. It was pretty handy when he was alone with his dick in his hand. Remembering Sorcha's shape, her smooth skin, the sound of her voice, was guaranteed to have him bowing off the bed within minutes. Now it was just inconvenient.

He sighed, planted his hands on his hips, and dropped his head as the true fuckedupness of the situation hit home. In this new position, he had the perfect view of the hard-on straining against the denim. His dick was looking for Sorcha. How was he supposed to go to that meeting when it would jump to attention the second she walked through the door?

Cisco's gaze followed Connor's, eyes widening as he appraised the situation.

"Dude." He forgot to use the bored, highbrow accent he usually affected. "Have you ever considered that there's a very basic solution to your situation?"

Connor turned to hail a cab. If he didn't think about Sorcha, the blood pooling between his legs would go back to where it would do him the most good—his brain. "What do you mean?"

This was idiotic. He shouldn't be thinking of sex now. A wyrm, maybe two, were out there, let loose on the unsuspecting public—unsupervised!

Maybe he was overreacting. Just because Raul hadn't answered his phone didn't mean that the worst had happened. There was every chance Raul was at home. Maybe his phone was buried under a pile of clothes and he hadn't heard it. Wyrms were notorious for avoiding laundry. Or maybe he was in the shower. Relief speared through him. The shower! Of course. That would explain everything.

He turned back to Cisco and caught the other man studying him with an air of consideration that sent warning bells to his brain.

"Just be reasonable," Cisco said. "This is a pesky hormonal issue, nothing more. You've wanted her for so long you've built her up in your mind to swimsuit model proportions. There's no way that Sorcha is worth what's going on with you. Just ask her out. Sleep with her. All it would take is one night, maybe two, to get her out of your system."

Connor was sure one *month*, maybe two, wouldn't be enough to purge the irritating Sorcha from his system.

"No."

"Connor, if you don't—"

"What did I just say?" Connor snapped, daring him to say another word.

Cisco lapsed into silence, though it was clear he wasn't finished.

Connor clenched his teeth and willed his flesh down.

Cisco thought Connor had a problem, and he did. There was not a man alive who wouldn't agree that a permanent hard-on around a particular woman was the most embarrassing thing that could happen, worse even than being turned down by said woman. But there was a reason Connor had avoided Sorcha all these years and that reason hadn't changed.

It was one, half-hour meeting. He could handle it. Just like he'd endured all the Christmas parties and other random meetings throughout the last five years.

And, if he was truthful, looked forward to like a lovesick, pathetic fool, even as he dreaded them.

A cab pulled up to the curb and they climbed in. Cisco slid to the opposite corner and reclined, arms crossed over his chest. Connor didn't like the way Cisco was contemplating him, like he was a room of furniture that needed to be rearranged.

Abruptly, Cisco leaned forward. "How long have you wanted this woman?"

Connor's lips tightened in irritation. "You know damn good and well how long. We were both in the same wyrm Guardian orientation session five years ago." He pushed himself deeper into the seat. "I don't want to talk about it."

The session where a girl with hair like silk and skin like cappuccino first took Connor to his knees.

"Look at Mr. Tall, Dark and Quiet," she'd said to him, while his brain had still been tangled from the first sight of her. "What's the matter? Cat got your tongue?"

What kind of woman opened up a conversation like that?

But she'd been just a girl then. And he'd been newly moved out of his parents' house, waiting for the day he would stop growing. Until he'd topped out at over six feet he'd never been comfortable with his proportions. Now his arms and legs moved when he told them to, but back then he'd been all gangly limbs, his height adding to his lack of grace. Boy, was that an understatement. He could stand ten feet away from a vase and knock it over. When he'd met Sorcha, he'd been overly sensitive, and Sorcha had nailed him in the gut with her mocking tone.

Cisco opened his mouth to speak, and Connor knew what was coming. More commentary on what Cisco considered his abysmal track record with women, and Sorcha in particular. But his friend was used to a different woman every week. He had no idea what it felt like to be so focused on one woman that it tied your stomach up in knots every time you saw her.

"I said no." He tried to forestall any more conversation on the subject with a hard glare. "If you value your manhood, drop it now."

"My manhood is of great value, certainly, but I'm afraid I can't leave it alone."

Connor wanted to bury his face in his hands. This was not good. Cisco with a mission was worse than a squirrel after a nut. He raised his chin and washed all emotion from his voice. "This is not your problem. Just let it go, okay?"

Silence. Those eyes were watching, and they had known Connor far too long to be fooled. Cisco's voice was quiet, reaching from the opposite depths of the cab as it bumped along the pot-holed city road. "She's in your blood. Isn't she?"

"I don't want her," he gritted.

Clearly a lie, but he desperately wanted it to be the truth. He'd say it all day if repetition would make it so. Say it just like he had, hard and cold, as if he could convince his body, his soul, to let Sorcha go.

And Cisco, damn his hide, knew it. He relaxed back, a faint smile curving across his otherwise serious face.

"Bob and weave, bob and weave, my friend." He turned to look at the passing traffic. "You can't hide from the truth. You've wanted her for years. I think this story's ending is already set in ink somewhere. There's no escaping it."

Connor turned to stare out his own window, shoulders hunched against Cisco's knowing gaze.

He muttered, "That's exactly what I'm afraid of."

☙❧

Damn! Damn! Damn!

Sorcha smiled to herself. It was so satisfying to curse.

Ladies didn't curse. Also, ladies didn't fight, ladies didn't drink. Ladies *did* have sex, but only in the missionary position. In the dark. With their clothes on.

Nobody had ever accused Sorcha of being a lady.

She stepped from the lobby into the elevator and jabbed a button. Recycled air hit her flushed cheeks as she watched the doors take an interminable time to slide together.

Hmmm. She could do better than damn, couldn't she? Especially if she was coming face to face with Connor McKenna in five minutes. What was worse than damn? A fuck, maybe. Yes, a fuck would be very dockworker. Connor would hate it.

Sorcha was old enough to know it wasn't normal, this urge to antagonize a perfectly nice and innocent human being. She suspected that it was a sign, in fact, that her psyche was seriously disturbed. But she couldn't turn it off, and honestly, was beyond caring. As far as she could tell, her mental health was perfectly fine except for one small glitch.

The desire to drive Connor McKenna crazy.

It didn't help that he made it so easy—mention the word breast or orgasm and he stalked away, lips thinned like she'd offended him to the soul. Thirty seconds and one well-placed dig and he was gone. But it wasn't all her fault. Oh, no. He provoked her just as much as she provoked him. Always so stiff, so standoffish, as if she had a disease he could catch just by talking to her. It was maddening.

Maybe with Raul and Louis both missing she'd give herself and Connor a break today. Keep her mouth busy with polite greetings and forget the buttons she could push that would send him into orbit.

As soon as the idea came, green eyes blazed through her memory, and she could feel the thrill that snaked down her spine when they pinned her with disapproval.

Okay, so maybe not.

Flicking a swathe of hair behind her shoulder, she looked down to make sure she wasn't falling out of her blouse. Some cleavage was good, necessary even, but she didn't want to come across as too tarty.

Sexy, intelligent. Untouchable.

Those would all do. She wanted Connor to look at her, see her, and want her. That wouldn't happen, so she'd settle for look at her, see her, and realize he'd been extremely, unforgivably wrong about her.

A ping, and the elevator opened onto the reception area of McPhail and Associates. Behind the curved desk, a sign displayed the name of the fictional company. If anybody got off on the wrong floor they would know that people in suits and ties worked here, believe that this was a completely normal business, not at all a secret organization that appointed Guardians to hundreds of wyrms all over the world and kept their existence a secret from mankind.

Stepping into the office, the emptiness reminded Sorcha of her first visit to McPhail and Associates. She'd been in culinary school at the time, and she'd answered an ad stapled to the bulletin board outside Á La Carte class. It promised a hundred dollars to anyone who would come in and take a series of tests, lasting no more than three hours. Several of her fellow students had answered the ad and vouched that it was no weird, guinea-pig-for-trial-medications deal, and she'd gone. Heck, a hundred dollars for one afternoon? A no brainer. Questions like "True or False, I believe that diversity is what makes this country great" made her wonder what exactly they were testing, but what did she care? She'd answered the questions, cashed the check, and hadn't thought any more of it—until they called her back for more testing, this time with a real person.

A gazillion psych profiles later, they'd offered her a job with the Directorate as a Guardian. Her response—hell, yes! She'd jumped at the honor, reveling in the Directorate's "sacred trust". Finally, something for herself, something her father and brothers couldn't take away from her for her own safety. Anyway, how cool was it to protect unsuspecting humans from the real life mythical creatures in their midst?

It had been thrilling to be included in a world where dragons and secret organizations existed outside of fiction novels. In the real world, Sorcha was a pastry chef at a four star restaurant, and though her job could be charged with adrenaline, it was hardly as vital as keeping Louis, a blue wyrm with raven dark hair and mommy issues, under control. People may say they needed her chocolate crème brulee with raspberry coulis, but they could live without it. What they couldn't survive was a wyrm on a rampage.

Wyrms had never overcome their thirteenth century mentality. They liked it there. It was comfortable. As far as a wyrm was concerned, it didn't get much better than sleeping in a cave, curled around a huge mound of gold and jewels, the peasants leaving offerings at their door.

Twenty-first century living was difficult for them, and they'd never acclimated. All the stimulation, all the excesses. The world was like a big carnival, with wild rides, decadent food, flashy signs, and it didn't take much before they were mesmerized and totally without impulse control.

Sorcha didn't know why this was, but she had a theory. Wyrms' brains, in their own form, were not proportional to the rest of their body. The big heavy torsos and wings dwarfed tiny heads perched atop long, dinosaur necks, leaving not much room for higher thinking in a brain the size of an orange.

In any case, the wyrms needed babysitters. Not every second—they weren't total vegetables—but more like a daily check-in. Someone needed to make sure that they hadn't maxed out their credit cards buying sparkly diamonds on QVC, or gorged themselves at the pastry shop, or found a willing partner and sexed themselves into a coma.

Sorcha had once heard of a wyrm that had taken human form and eaten its way through five Starbucks in an hour's time. By the time they'd got to him, the stores were cleaned out—the pastries, the coffee, the whipped cream...everything. The wyrm had been so hyped on caffeine and sugar he'd been breathing fire. Only tiny puffs on each exhale, but they were still lucky there had been no damage and that no one had gone to the tabloids.

In Sorcha's mind, that was a prime example of why the thirteenth century with its cave dwelling was better for everybody, wyrms and humans. But you couldn't turn back the clock; you could only deal with what was.

Lately, Sorcha had become aware of a restlessness inside herself, an itch that told her maybe it was time to move on. The wyrms were starting to get on her nerves. Louis could be more trouble than infant triplets. She felt like a harried mother with an egregiously precocious child, and while it was one thing to make sure a toddler didn't fall down the stairs, it was another thing entirely to fish gold coins out of a toilet because a wyrm thought it was the ideal place to keep his horde.

If she was truthful with herself, she knew if not for Connor she would have quit and gone on with her life a long time ago. But the only connection she had to him was the Directorate, and if she were no longer a Guardian she wouldn't have an excuse to see him again. The thought of cutting all ties made her palms sweat and her chest fill up with black goo, and she was coward enough to put off making the decision. Just a little while longer.

In the main hallway now, she walked quickly to the Director's office and stopped outside the partially open door. She was purposefully five minutes late. The Director was staring across the desk at someone, curled index finger tapping slowly on a file in the center of his desk.

Connor. She could feel him. Slouched in his seat, knees spread, taking up more than his fair share of space. Feeling a surge of anticipation, Sorcha rapped on the doorframe and stepped into the small room. "I'm not interrupting, am I?"

The Director motioned towards an empty seat. "Come in, Sorcha. Sit down."

She slid next to Connor, making her movements deliberate and steady. The last thing she wanted was to appear flustered around Connor McKenna. Slowly, she brought up one leg, bare and silky in a black mini, and crossed it over the other. Could Connor hear the faint rasp of bare skin on bare skin?

Connor stared forward, hands fisted on huge thighs. With his hair tucked untidily behind his ears, she could see flags of color darkening his sharp cheekbones. Well-muscled shoulders jutted out on either side of the chair and his knees shot several inches over the seat.

The Director closed the file and eased back in his chair. He leveled his gaze. "Sorcha. How long has it been since you've seen or talked with Louis?"

With an effort, she dragged her attention away from Connor and forced it to the matter at hand.

"Yesterday evening I went by his apartment and he was there," she said. "Today he was going to watch his soaps and then go shopping for ski-ware. I'm not even sure I would say he's missing, but he wasn't at home when the alert came around, and he's not answering his cell."

"Is that unusual?"

"No. Even if he has it with him he usually forgets to charge it and the batteries are usually dead."

The Director transferred his hard gaze. "Connor? What about Raul?"

"I checked his apartment earlier, and he wasn't there. Um...Sunday was the last time I saw him. I haven't talked to him since."

"Sunday!" Sorcha's spine separated from the back of the chair. "That's nearly a week ago! What have you been doing that you haven't checked on Raul in a week?"

Connor flushed, the muscles in his jaw taut.

"I was busy," he muttered, flicking her a dark glance. "We haven't had any trouble out of Raul in months. I thought he finally understood that he needed to be more circumspect with his activities."

"Connor McKenna, everybody knows you can't trust a wyrm to make their bed if there's not a reward involved. To expect Raul, the flightiest—"

"Enough." The hard press of his lips showed the Director wasn't happy with Connor, but his tone was even. "Connor, I don't think I have to tell you that's not the best decision you ever made, but it's too late to do anything about it now.

"Here's the situation. It's come to our attention that an aphrodisiac is being sold down on High Street. It goes by the street name Bliss. Normally, this wouldn't be a cause for alarm, because those things are usually a hit and run racket. Drop a bunch of fake merchandise then get the hell out of Dodge before the law, or your customers, catch up with you. This time, it's the real thing."

"How do you know?" The stoic expression on the Director's face intrigued Sorcha. The man never cracked a smile, but now he seemed almost...pained.

"There's been a rash of couples admitted to emergency rooms throughout the city. The males are chronically tumescent and both parties are rubbed raw on their...er...privates. There's been bleeding, dehydration, exhaustion, and yet the couples are still compelled to have intercourse. Bliss is the real deal. And, unfortunately, the Directorate knows where it's coming from."

The chair creaked as Connor leaned forward. "Where?"

The Director sighed and rubbed his forehead, where deep lines etched in the skin made him look weary. "From a wyrm. It's not widely known in the Directorate, but a wyrm's semen, when shot into a human's bloodstream, is a potent aphrodisiac. It can turn one orgasm into multiples. It can make sex last for days. The only problem is, it's addictive. And a health hazard.

Just ask those people in the emergency rooms. Once someone has sex while on Bliss, they'll always want to have sex with Bliss, and they'll want to have sex all the time. When I put together the symptoms and the drug, I knew we had a missing wyrm. Now we've narrowed it down to Louis and Raul."

Sorcha had a thought. "How long has this Bliss been on the street?"

"About three days."

"Then I doubt it's Louis."

The Director nodded. "You're probably right. But we have to be sure."

"Wait a minute," Connor said. "Who else knows about these special properties?"

"The wyrms know. And a few other Directorate personnel, all of whom have been checked out. But it's not common knowledge and I...well, I'm worried. I think someone kidnapped Raul...or Louis...thinking he was a rich human and they could demand a large ransom. Somehow...I don't know how...they've realized they have a wyrm. Maybe they tortured him, were able to drug him. Somehow they discovered the special properties of the wyrm's semen and have figured out a way to make a profit."

After this statement, he paused to let the information sink in.

Sorcha shook her head, imagining the torture Raul must have suffered to give up his most precious secret. "Poor Raul. We have to find him."

She didn't know Raul very well. Wyrms were antisocial by nature. Solitary creatures, they usually allowed their Guardian to handle everything outside their home, and were happy to do so. She could imagine Raul—naked, chained to a wall, drugged. The thought of how they were using the poor wyrm made her angry. And it was all Connor's fault.

If Connor had been doing his job they would have known Raul was missing days ago. Sorcha threw Connor a scathing look. How could he be so irresponsible?

The Director continued. "This is our worst case scenario. We know someone has a wyrm somewhere, and that they know it's a wyrm. They're making a lot of money off Bliss and they're not going to want to give that up. It's our responsibility to stop them."

Sorcha crossed her arms over her chest. She leaned over long enough to hiss, "Connor, how could you?"

He ignored her. He'd barely looked at her since she'd come into the room. Connor was treating her no differently than he ever had. Why, out of all the men on the planet, did she have to want him, the one man who couldn't care less whether she was alive or dead?

It was twisted. It was sick.

She'd been drawn to Connor from the moment she'd first laid eyes on him. He'd been smiling at something Cisco had said, lips curved, eyes laughing. One thing you knew about Connor right away—what you saw was what you got. He never put on an act or tried to be something he wasn't.

Sorcha was drawn to that, drawn to the fact that he wasn't a strutting peacock with more aggression than sense, as most of the men in her life had been. And physically it didn't hurt that he was an excellent specimen. Thick muscles sat on a huge frame. With his shoulder length hair she could easily imagine him charging into battle, face contorted, the massive muscles of his thighs bunching and releasing as he pushed forward. A warrior.

Noble. Honorable. Implacable. That was Connor.

That first time, flustered at the sight of his strong, serious face and deep green eyes, she'd blabbed the first thing that came into her head. Connor had that affect on her. Something short-circuited in her brain around him and all coolness fled.

But he...well, he had disliked her on sight. And she didn't understand why. What was wrong with her? Why did he laugh and joke with every other Guardian but clam up the moment she came close to him?

It. Made. Her. Crazy.

The only way she could drag a response out of him was to act out like a three-year-old. So she did. And she'd continue as long as it meant those emerald eyes would fall on her, even in censure.

She was pathetic.

The Director said, "Listen up. You two are going to find the missing wyrm."

"What!" Connor jerked bolt upright.

"Sorcha," the Director went on, "I know what you're thinking, but I'm not discounting Louis's involvement in this."

Sorcha knew which wyrm was missing, but she didn't argue. Time would tell. Anyway, she was trying not to flush with pleasure. Her and Connor, working together. A whole afternoon, a whole evening. Who knew how long it would take?

As she said a mixed thank you and prayer to Raul, she realized Connor wasn't as pleased with the idea of working together as she was. In fact, he was staring at her with horror in his eyes.

Reality slammed into her sternum and the blood drained from her face. "That's not very flattering, Connor." Pride kept her tone even, though her lips felt numb. "For God's sake, I'm not an asp."

Immediately he attempted to school his features, but it was too late. Pain reverberated in her chest, the swell growing larger with each passing second.

"Uh...that's not what—"

She crossed her arms over the worst of the pain. "Whatever."

Connor would have spoken again, probably to apologize, because he was at most a nice, upstanding guy. It wasn't his fault they weren't compatible. She didn't blame him for not thinking she was the greatest thing since peanut butter.

"Do you guys need a time out?" The Director's sarcasm intruded into her misery. "Now, we're all adults here. I think. Connor, do you have a problem working with Sorcha?"

Painfully aware of his reluctance, she stared straight ahead. Out of the corner of her eye she saw him shift in his seat. There was no good reason he could give for refusing to work with her, and he knew it. He slouched back, knees falling wide—my God, the man would take up a whole sofa—and threw her a cautious look. "No."

"Sorcha?"

"Works for me, boss," she said in her best flippant tone. Maybe she should take these feelings as a sign. All this hurt and misery swelling in her skin—it was *not* okay. She yearned for Connor, but she wasn't a masochist.

Connor didn't want her, end of story. No more teasing, no more provoking, just no more. Because *it didn't work*. She'd been living in a dream world, hoping if she pushed him hard enough, long enough, Connor would wake up and see her.

It would never happen.

Or maybe he had seen her, and the truth was he just didn't like the view.

Sorcha gathered herself and walked out of the office. She was beyond tears. She was beyond anything but a huge tidal wave of anger, all of it aimed at herself. Five years spent pining over a self-involved oaf. Five years she could never get back living in some unattainable dream. All that time and what did she have to show for it? A lot of lonely nights and a feeling of unworthiness.

So what if he was the best man she'd ever known. So what if he was gorgeous.

Connor McKenna wasn't for her.

Chapter Two

Connor knew he'd screwed up.

They were in the elevator. Since they'd left the Director's office, Sorcha had refused to look at him.

Trying not to appear like he was staring, he watched her from the corner of his eye. Face impassive, she stared up at the flashing numbers, her petite form stiff. He opened his mouth, but couldn't think of what to say. Shutting it again, he shot furtive glances at her firm jaw, wishing the ride to the lobby were longer.

He hadn't meant to be insulting. But she'd walked in and the cloud of Sorcha scent had permeated the room. It had gone to his head. And his dick. He'd felt like a caged animal in the confined space, instincts yelling at him to run, to escape, to jump on her.

Of course, that wasn't an excuse. That was just his own weakness, and it wasn't her fault he'd acted like an ass.

The doors opened and Sorcha took off. Connor lagged behind, taking the opportunity to get an eyeful of her lean, muscular legs and the trim body she kept toned to battle the indulgences of her profession.

Appreciation filled him at her grace. She strode away, every click of her heels a rebuke. Some women couldn't walk in heels. They minced along on the balls of their feet as if placing their body weight on the stilettos would cause them to slide right out from under them. Not Sorcha. She wore the heels with authority, and he had a feeling she could go rock climbing in those things if she wanted.

Usually he tried not to look at Sorcha. Whenever his gaze lingered on her for more than a second, he tended to get tunnel vision. Time was lost. Conversations were tuned out. It was embarrassing. He'd come to once or twice to find Cisco staring at him, his friend's wry expression telling him he'd been buried in watching her smile, her eyes, so deeply that for a moment he'd been pulled out of the world.

So he'd stopped looking, and considered it a fit punishment for lusting after a woman who thought he was a boring tightass. It was for the better, anyway. Sorcha could never catch him staring like a moon-eyed youth. The cut down that would follow would emasculate him for the rest of his life.

But when she'd walked into the office today, he hadn't been able to resist stealing a glance at her. She wore a v-neck blouse that exposed the upper quadrants of her breasts. Black and white striped ruffles climbed the edges where it wrapped around her torso, complementing the narrow black skirt hugging the curve of her hips. She kept herself in excellent shape. However, genes were genes and there were some things she couldn't firm up, couldn't alter, and because of this Connor knew God was a man. Sorcha's breasts and ass would always bounce.

Over the years he'd soaked up countless details of her habits and dress without even realizing it. He knew she didn't like to wear jewelry. Occasionally she threaded golden hoops in her lobes, but her nimble fingers were always free of rings. He knew she kept them clean so they wouldn't interfere with her work.

He loved those hands, and couldn't find one fault with the rest of her. Sorcha's skin was the color of café au lait, smooth and unblemished. Her soft eyes reflected caramel in the sun. She wore her chocolate hair parted on the side, large curls left free to bounce around her shoulders and her breasts.

Connor raked a hand through his hair. Christ, he needed to get a hold of himself. He'd never spent so much time thinking about a woman. Likening her hair to food. Remembering her smile. Wondering what she looked like naked.

But he couldn't seem to help himself. How could he? Sorcha was fire and heat, her humor and smile always flashing, her sexy, gurgling laugh spearing right to his groin.

But she wasn't smiling now, was she?

Connor pushed open the glass door and hit the street, sun and fresh air washing over him.

He didn't like feeling he'd fucked up royally. It was no secret he and Sorcha rubbed each other the wrong way. Anybody who had ever spent more than a minute with the two of them knew they were like a cat and a dog trapped together in a sack.

So why, deep inside, did he want to fall at her feet and grovel until she gave him one of those warm, Sorcha smiles?

He spotted her ten yards away, a lone, beautiful woman on a teeming city street. Jogging, he caught up and clamped a hand on her elbow, forcing her to a halt.

She swung around, reluctance clear on her face.

Connor sucked in a bracing breath, prepared to apologize. "Hey—"

Brown eyes, usually soft and liquid, were like permafrost. He hadn't known brown could be icy. "Forget it, Connor."

"But I want—"

"I don't want to hear it."

"Sorcha, would you just—"

"Shut up! Just shut up!" Sorcha leaned towards him until they were one unit for the steady stream of pedestrians to flow around. "I get it, okay? There's nothing to apologize for. Not liking me is not a crime." Her lips twisted wryly. "Don't shred your tender heart for me. If you'll notice, right now you're not on my list of favorite people either. But it doesn't matter. Let's just find the missing wyrm so this will all be over with."

Sorcha's anger brought the blush back to her skin. The faint breeze blew strands of dark hair across her cheek and lips.

Connor wanted to have the right to reach out and brush the hair away.

He wanted to throw a blanket over her. She was showing too much of her body, and only he should be the one to see, to know how beautiful she was.

He wanted to be inside of her. It would be hot there, sizzling.

Today, more than ever, the rejection of these feelings tore at him, raged inside him. How much longer could he deny them?

It was like the words came from a different person. "You're showing too much skin," Connor said. "Your shirt is cut down to your navel."

Oh, great, Connor. Insult her again, why don't you? He braced himself. Sorcha had a tongue like a wasp and never thought twice about using it, especially on him. And this time he deserved it.

She didn't say a word. She simply stood there, like a remote statue, freezing him out.

He stared at her, thrown. Where was Sorcha? Where was the fire, the vibrancy?

"Are you quite finished?" Clipped and final, the words chilled him.

A shoulder rose in defense. "Sorry," he muttered, stung.

Sorcha took a deep breath, blew it out. She shook herself, and he could see her throwing off the tension and acclimating herself to the world beyond the two of them. "Where do you think we should start?"

Start? Who cared where they started? Why wouldn't she argue with him? "Um..."

He looked at her helplessly. What had been the question?

Shaking her head as if she were the most unfortunate woman on earth, she said. "Okay. Let's split up. You check Raul's apartment one more time. I'll go to Louis's. If we find either at home, great. If we don't, we can snoop and maybe find a clue as to where they might be. Let's meet at the diner on Fifth Street in one hour." She turned to go.

A solid, reasonable plan.

"No," he said.

Sorcha swiveled back to face him. "What? Why not?"

All right. Now you have to think of a reason. Why? Why? "The Director wants us to work together."

As justifications went, it was weak as runny oatmeal. Sorcha would know it, too.

She stopped, placed one hand on her hip and cocked her head. "Connor, are you okay?"

"Why do you ask?"

"You're acting...bizarre."

"I'm fine."

She snorted. "So *you* say. Why do you want to stick together when we could cover twice as much ground apart? We need to split up."

Plus, he suspected, she was trying to get rid of him. Well, he wasn't about to let her go so easily.

"I've already been to Raul's apartment today."

"I know," she said, "But he could be home now. Raul's apartment is across town. If Louis isn't home, we'll just have to trek all the way over there. This way, we can each go to our wyrm's apartment and call each other to see what we've found. It'll save us time."

He cast around desperately for another excuse, and all he could come up with was, "I don't have my cell phone."

She looked at him strangely. "Raul's got a phone in his house, doesn't he? Use that one."

For a second, he considered telling her it had been disconnected, then decided he didn't want her thinking he hadn't been making sure Raul's bills were paid on time and discarded the idea. Then he was hit with inspiration.

"I could just call him."

"You could, but I know for a fact that Raul doesn't always answer his phone. If he doesn't, you'll still have to go over there just to be sure."

She had him there. It felt different, being on the other side of logic. Usually he was the reasonable one, the calm one. All he could do was push and hope she didn't notice he wasn't making a lot of sense. "It could be dangerous," he said, jaw hardening as he prepared to fight to the bitter end. "We need to stick together."

Now she would blow up, tell him what an idiot he was. That she could take care of herself and didn't need a man along to make sure she was safe. She would call him a cretinous barbarian and insult his mother.

Finally, she just sighed and said, “Whatever. Let’s just get this over with.” She took off down the street, each round ass cheek dropping as she walked. “Louis’s apartment is closest. Let’s go there first.” Stopping short, she turned and surveyed him with raised eyebrows. “If that’s okay with you?”

He nodded, his features schooled, as they always were around her. It was instinct, an animal drive for self-preservation.

Usually he was shielding her from his lust, but now he had another emotion he couldn’t allow her to see. A feeling caused not so much *by* her as of the thought of never seeing her again.

It was a feeling Connor hadn’t known often, but it bit at him now, sharp and cold, spreading through his blood.

Oh, he had a feeling all right. And it was fear.

ଓଓଌଌ

Louis lived in a deluxe penthouse a few blocks away. Sorcha let them into the spacious foyer after knocking for a good five minutes with no response.

“Louis? Are you here?”

Sorcha’s voice echoed back from the marble floors. Connor had never been in Louis’s apartment before. It was luxurious and spacious, but with a hollow feel, as if the apartment wished for more than one occupant.

“Empty,” Connor said.

Sorcha stepped into the belly of the apartment, her heels tapping on the floor. “Let’s look around and see if we find anything suspicious. A half an hour, okay? Then we'll go to Raul's."

The living room and dining room were tidy, but stale. When they stepped into the kitchen, Connor's first thought was, *here's a room that's lived in.* His second was, *it's such a mess, who would want to*?

Dishes filled the sink and the garbage can overflowed. Connor wasn't surprised, but it was a shame Louis couldn't take the time to load the dishwasher or wipe the crumbs from the counter in his gourmet kitchen. Sorcha probably sent a cleaning service by once or twice a week to keep the place from becoming a health code violation.

Sorcha made a token effort to sift through the trash, but gave up two layers down at the slimy Chinese takeout containers. Turning to the overflowing sink, she threw up her hands in dismay.

"Darn it, Louis." Sorcha reached over the sink and picked up a tiny spider plant in a green plastic container.

Connor walked up beside her. "What idiot gave Louis a plant?"

"I did," Sorcha said, wrenching the faucet on and shoving the poor plant under the flowing stream. Water immediately began pouring out the bottom, the soil too dry to hold it.

He looked at the half dead thing. All the bladelike leaves had spiky ends tipped in brown, and some were shriveled down to the dirt. "That thing needs to be in plant ICU."

Setting the plant in the sink, Sorcha opened the cabinet underneath. "I know. It's just... There's not one living thing in this apartment besides Louis. I thought he might like having something green and fresh around. It was an idiotic impulse."

Lips quirking, Connor watched her poke around under the sink. "At least you didn't give him a puppy."

Sorcha glanced up, smiling. “No. Next, I was bringing him a fish. I guess that’s out now. Where’s his plant food? Doesn’t everyone keep their plant food under the sink?”

“I wouldn’t know.” Connor didn’t. Like Louis, he didn’t have any plants. He couldn’t remember to water the darned things, and even when he did, he either watered them too much or too little and they died anyway.

He smiled bemusedly at her dark head. Only Sorcha would try to give a wyrm a plant, something that needed a little tending, a little attention. It was optimistic of her, but seriously misguided.

With a sigh, Sorcha closed the cabinet and stood. “Forget it. I’ll take the poor thing home. It might recover with some TLC.”

Connor doubted it, but kept quiet.

They decided to hit the bedroom next. Sorcha led the way to a room decorated in black and gold. As he approached, his nose retreated from the sickly sweet smell of the sandalwood cologne Louis used. The scent was so intense, the curtains and sheets probably smelled of it straight from the dryer.

He held back in the doorway while Sorcha moved towards the nightstand. Straight ahead, the bed was a flat plate of gold. On the right, two doors interrupted the wall, a bathroom and another, closed door, which he assumed was the closet.

The room was small compared to the rest of the apartment, but the bed was huge. Big enough to fit a wyrm in its natural form.

Suddenly, Connor’s thoughts veered out of his control. *Sorcha* and *bed,* two objects so often together in his imagination, were right in front of him. In the same room. Inches apart.

He hardened instantly, overwhelmed with the urge to take Sorcha down. For a moment, he thought he'd actually done it. He came to himself, hands shaking, a door barely an inch from his nose. Good. His instincts had kicked in and he'd turned his back on Sorcha when his body reacted to her presence. It was an old habit. God knew how many conversations he'd had with her over his shoulder as he waited for an erection to subside.

"Connor? Connor?" Sorcha's voice sought him. By the raised pitch he realized this wasn't the first time she'd spoke to him while he'd struggled with his baser urges.

"Connor?"

His erection pulsed beneath his zipper. He dared not turn around. Sorcha would see the effect she had on him and would no doubt laugh and make some crude remark. He wanted—no—he needed her. But he was also scared to death of her and the damage she could do once she ripped through his heart. Hurricane Sorcha.

Muffled footsteps crossed the room behind him. "Dammit, Connor!"

Connor jerked open the closet door and began pushing past Louis's three thousand dollar suits.

Sorcha's annoyed voiced followed. "What's wrong with you? Why won't you answer me?"

"Nothing," he said, trying to sound cool. Stretching out his arms, he felt for the light switch he knew was back at the door. "I'm just checking out the closet, see?"

No response. Connor looked over his shoulder. She wasn't following him, thank God. She'd stopped at the entrance to the big walk-in closet like it was a door to an evil kingdom.

"You better get out of there." She shifted nervously. "Louis wouldn't want you in his closet."

"Why not?"

"Uh-uh. I'm not gonna say. That's patient/client privilege. If I tell you, he'll never forgive me."

Wooden hangers rattled as his palms passed over racks and racks of wool slacks, silk ties, and cashmere. A loafer obstacle course made navigating difficult because it was too dark to see his feet. The light from the room penetrated only a few feet into the deep closet.

"Sorcha, there is no such thing as patient/client privilege. We're glorified babysitters, not doctors."

Sorcha sighed, glanced quickly over her shoulder. Shaking her head and muttering unintelligibly, she waded in after him.

"Shows how much you know," she said, feeling her way with her feet. "Louis and I get along because I understand him. He has boundaries, secrets, just like anyone else, and he trusts me. Now come on. Get out of here."

She closed in on him and heat wreathed his back. Wrapping her hands around his right biceps, she tugged, trying to pull him back into the light.

She was only trying to get him out of the closet. His brain knew that.

But all his body knew was Sorcha...Sorcha!...was voluntarily touching him. Through the fabric of his T-shirt, on his bare skin, he felt each slender finger like a brand.

His dick, a maverick unit, understood her touch to be an invitation and grew even harder.

It was no wonder he'd avoided her all these years. Connor was used to having complete control over his baser urges. He had a strong sex drive, sure, but he didn't have to have sex.

But Sorcha shattered his control, snapped it as if it were the ethereal filament of a spider's web. Whenever she was around, his libido was on constant alert.

"Connor, I mean it. Let's go." She tugged harder. He stood firm, like an oak tree. He would move when he was damn good and ready. If only she would leave, then his mind would clear and he wouldn't embarrass himself.

Suddenly she was pressed against his back, soft breasts, flat stomach, the scent of her piercing his brain. She was still trying to turn him, one hand on his right shoulder pulling him around, the other pushing his hip. And, oh, God, she was shoving her hip into his left side, using her body to maneuver him.

Connor's fingers clenched involuntarily at the contact. Then he lost it. He whipped around, reaching out to touch her, to finally put his hands on that creamy flesh.

"Oomph!" He tripped over something hard and irregular.

Connor didn't fall, but Sorcha did, propelled by his shoulder. He immediately lost her in the black nothing coating the floor. Crouching, he followed her down, the press of clothes and shoes more oppressive here. He carefully searched the dark air with his hands, silently praying to connect with something innocuous like an elbow or a nose. A light touch grazed the back of his hand. Her hair.

"Are you all right?"

She brushed his hands away. "I'm fine. Let's just get out of here. If Louis comes home and finds us in his closet he'll have a hissy."

"Louis can go stuff himself." Easing onto his knees, Connor felt for the misplaced object, but there was more than one. If these shoes weren't cleared away, Sorcha could hurt herself.

On his hands and knees, he scooped shoes to either side of the closet, uncaring of the jumble he was making of them. He reached out, expecting a man's boring, rectangular shoe to hit his palm. A stiletto heel stabbed him.

"What the hell?"

Sweeping the thing up, he held it up to the light. A strappy woman's shoe, black, with a reflective silver lining and tiny rhinestone straps.

"Uh-oh." In front of him, Sorcha whispered under her breath.

Connor's vision blacked out, then flashed to red. He couldn't feel his hand, but could see it was trembling, the edges of the shoe cutting deep into his palm. His calmness surprised him, as did the eerie, dead quality of his voice. "What. Have you. Done."

"Nothing. What do you mean? Nothing." A nervous laugh bubbled like cheap champagne.

He couldn't see Sorcha, only an indistinct shape on the floor. Nothing in his life had prepared him for the piercing depth of the pain of this moment.

Women's shoes in Louis's closet. Sorcha wore shoes like these. Strappy and sexy were her trademark. His mind leapt the small distance between suspicion and dreadful truth.

"These are your shoes." The words were raw, grating. "You're sleeping with Louis."

She'd had lovers, of course she had. Why not? He had. He'd never expected Sorcha to go without sex.

But he'd blocked all thoughts of other men right out of his brain. There were no boyfriends, no dates, no lovers. He wouldn't allow himself to even go there.

But he couldn't hold his head in the sand any longer. Sorcha had a lover. And it was a wyrm.

"I am not sleeping with Louis!" She had the nerve to sound shocked.

His lip curled. "Please. These are yours. Who else would they belong to?"

He couldn't see her, but her exasperation was evident in her voice. "I don't know," she huffed, "how about any other woman on the planet?"

Sorcha tried to retreat, but she was turned sideways. Behind her a wall of shoeboxes and tightly packed slacks blocked her way. She twisted and the muted light from the door washed over her face. Scowling fiercely, she planted her feet on his chest and pushed, heels digging divots in his muscles.

He didn't move.

She dropped her legs with a sigh. "Connor, I do not understand the way your mind works. You find shoes in Louis's closet and immediately assume they're mine? Are you kidding? For a handler to sleep with their wyrm is just so...*sketch*!" Palms down, she cut the air in a negative gesture.

He wasn't sure he believed her. And while he thought those shoes were hers, he absolutely had to have her in this position. Sorcha reclining before him in a posture of submission set off his possessive instincts like nothing else.

"You want me to prove it to you?" she said. "All right."

She pressed her heel into the carpet, loosening her shoe. Kicking it off, she leaned back on her elbows and raised her leg. Her stomach muscles were amazing. She showed no signs of strain as she balanced on her butt, leg extended, toes inches from his nose. "Let's try the thing on then. Come on, just like Cinderella's glass slipper."

Though she wasn't straining, the position couldn't be easy to hold. In an instinctive movement, Connor cupped the back of her thigh, the smooth skin right behind her knee like silk.

Fuck. His thigh muscles started to quiver, and his erection was beginning to hurt. Sorcha was splayed open before him, sumptuous and female.

In seconds, he could be inside her. It would take minimal preparation. Push her leg to the side, leaving her open and exposed. Tear away whatever piece of lace and fluff passed for panties. Release his erection and be buried in her wetness.

Connor realized he was sweating, and shook his head to clear it. Whoa, whoa. Who said she was wet?

She was simply offering to prove something to him and he was out of control.

The hand behind her knee slid to her ankle. He slid the shoe on.

It hung off her foot like a little girl wearing her mother's high heels. The damn thing was five sizes too big.

His mind stuttered over the information. "I don't get it."

Sorcha retrieved her foot. She reached down and the shoe hit the carpet with a muffled thunk. "It's Louis's."

"Louis's girlfriend has feet as big as mine?"

She hissed in exasperation. "No, the shoe *belongs* to Louis. As in, he wears it. Louis likes to wear women's shoes. It's his deep, dark secret and he'd kill me if anyone ever found out, so you have to keep your mouth shut, do you hear me Connor McKenna? Promise me. Swear it."

"I swear."

"Good. Now let's get this mess cleaned up and get out of here. He could come home any minute."

Scrambling onto her hands and knees, she excavated shoes from the piles he'd made of them, matching and shoving them up against the rows of shoeboxes.

Her ass was on prominent display. The skirt rose on her hips and he could see the dark, warm place between her legs. When she would turn this way or that, her breasts would sway gently, and he held back a groan.

"Damn wyrm has more shoes than I do," she grumbled, holding a peach slingback with beaded tassels in one hand as she searched for its mate. "And nicer ones, too. It's a crime to own Manolos and not take them out in public. If we were the same size—"

"Sorcha?"

She looked up, a distracted frown marring her smooth forehead.

"What?"

"I'm going to kiss you now."

She froze.

He cupped her elbows and pulled her to her knees. Her hair caught on the fabric of his sleeves, curled around his wrist, dark sable in the dim light.

"You've got ten seconds to tell me no."

She'd stopped breathing. Just stared up at him with rounded eyes.

"Nine. Eight..."

Chapter Three

Connor waited, hands resting lightly on her shoulders. He was treading on dangerous ground, balanced on a pinnacle high above boiling hot lava. One misstep in any direction and it was over, but it didn't matter. He couldn't go on anymore pretending he didn't want her.

She hadn't said anything. Not a "Hell, yes!" not a "Get away from me!" What was going on in her head? Was she shocked? Horrified?

He was tired of pining. He wanted to take. If she slapped his pride with an open palm, so be it. But if she refused him...Connor didn't know what would happen. Yes, he did. He would kiss her anyway. He had to, just to know. If he was lucky it would be like kissing an anteater.

Dammit to hell and back, what was she thinking?

Sorcha's head fell back, exposing her smooth throat. Her hair hung behind her like licks of dark flame. Dewy lips parted, brown eyes softened.

And Connor knew what it meant.

He lunged for her mouth and, with a groan of animal pleasure, pulled her close, the front line of her body searing through his clothes, pressing against his aching erection.

He cut his lips across hers, and plunged his tongue into her mouth. In the back of his mind he knew he was being rough, squeezing her shoulders with his thick fingers, forcing her jaw wide. Sorcha fisted his T-shirt, jerked, as if it were the only thing holding her upright. She leaned against him, into his body, like a flower towards the sun.

She dragged her lips off his long enough to whisper against his mouth, "I am furious with you, Connor McKenna."

He persisted with deep, wet kisses. "Why?"

"This." She reached down to cup his erection. There was no way she could have missed it, the thing was as big as a baseball bat. "This is for me, isn't it?"

He sucked in his breath on a wave of pleasure, and rocked his hips forward, pressing himself into her palm. "For as long as I can remember." God, when had his voice grown so ragged?

"Why?"

She tasted like cinnamon, fiery and soothing at the same time. "What?" Her mouth was like a savored treat, and she was keeping it from him. He dove to her neck, teeth scraping lightly.

"I don't understand. Why?"

How could he explain the need, the doubt?

Connor pulled back, resting his forehead against hers. He laughed, but it was a choked, self-deprecating sound. Which answer should he give her? He had a whole bag of them. They'd propped him up for years, but now none of them were worth a damn. Because he'd wanted her forever. Because she could be the toughest, yet kindest person he knew. Because she could take a day and make it worthwhile just by walking in a room.

"Because..."

He would never say any of it.

Sorcha reached up, lacing her fingers through the untidy hanks of hair on either side of his face. She tugged him down until their lips were an inch apart.

"I am furious with you," she said again. Only she didn't sound furious. She sounded breathy and aroused. "And later on we are going to discuss how you could torture both of us the way you have and what in the world held you back. But right now, I just want you inside me."

Blood roared in his ears as he pressed her back on the carpet. Enough of his sanity remained for him to know he needed to be gentle, but he wasn't sure he could be. He'd wanted this so long it was almost like a dream, and as he bunched her skirt around her waist and ripped off her thong, it was with hands that shook.

He started to remove her shirt, but when his hands slid under the hem and encountered bare skin, his purpose faltered. Her skin was cool compared to the heat leaching from his, her smoothness an oasis. He couldn't believe this was real.

Breath rasped in his throat and the tight grip of his control deteriorated. To buy some time he buried his face in her neck, but she squirmed underneath him. Dammit, if she didn't hold still he was going to come in his pants.

"Be still," he commanded.

She surged under him. "No."

Loath to let her go for even a moment, Connor released the catch of her bra one-handed. He managed to remove that and her blouse with an arm wrapped around her waist, fusing their lower bodies.

Finally he lay between her thighs. Her nipples were rose, tiny ripe raspberries. He laved one with his tongue. It pearled tight and Sorcha arched under him, offering more.

Her hands roamed restlessly under his shirt, searching every inch of bare skin. She forced the fabric up, gathering it in his armpits, then rubbed her stomach and ribs over his like a cat. God, this was incredible, *she* was incredible.

Pressure gathered between his legs, building to an almost unbearable degree and leaving him on the brink of explosion. It didn't help that an ongoing chant in his brain kept reminding him that the half-naked woman in his arms was Sorcha. *Sorcha.* With a will born of desperation, he clenched his teeth against the rising tide of his orgasm.

Sweat pooled in the small of his back. To test her readiness, he slid a hand between her legs. Instead of curls, his finger encountered slick, plump lips. She was absolutely bare. He hissed as his cock jerked towards her like a homing beacon. "Holy hell, Sorcha," he choked.

Connor's entire body began to tremble. He needed to pull back, retrench. But he couldn't remove his hand from her folds, couldn't release the visual in his head of pouting lips, slick with need. The bottom of the closet was airless, but he didn't need air. He didn't need to breathe. He needed Sorcha.

Arms twined around his neck, and her lips brushed the rim of his ear. "Now," she whispered.

In point four seconds his cock was released from his jeans, and he spent an agonizing moment fishing for a condom and rolling it on. Finally, finally, oh God help him, he positioned himself at her entrance, lodging just the tip.

He was big. He couldn't help it; his body was proportional. He needed to be gentle with Sorcha. However, his body was objecting to the thought of slow and easy. It was ready to ram into her and come out the other side. His mind was the voice of reason. It said, "This is Sorcha." Because it was her, it was enough to turn him into a ravening, lustful animal. But because it was her, it gave him the strength to hold himself back.

Experimentally he circled his hips. Even wet as she was, it was a tight fit.

“Okay?” he rasped.

“More,” she demanded, raising her hips and sheathing another inch of hard flesh.

A strangled laugh escaped. That was his Sorcha, all right. “Honey, I don’t want to hurt you.”

“You couldn’t. Not ever. Please, Connor, I’m burning up.”

With one thrust, he sheathed himself entirely. She was tight, and oh, so hot. She was right—she was burning, she was fire, she was everything good under the sun.

Moaning, she climaxed immediately, internal muscles clenching him like a fist. “Holy hell,” he muttered. With those pulses urging him on, Connor lost control.

Hands planted on either side of her head, he held himself at the top of a push-up and drove into her. Hips swinging as fast as pistons, each thrust elicited a squeak as Sorcha rocked on the carpet. Fingers dug into his buttocks and urged him closer, deeper. Every muscle in her body tightened as she fought for another orgasm. “Oh, please. Oh, please,” she whispered.

Connor’s spine tingled as his control reached its limit. Folding onto his elbows, he lifted trembling hands to smooth dark strands of hair from her forehead. He brushed a thumb under her jaw. “Look at me."

The light from the bedroom slanted over her face. Long lashes drifted up, revealing chocolate brown eyes. “Connor.” A whisper of satisfaction that had nothing to do with sex.

It seemed as if he'd been waiting his whole life to be just in this place, with this woman. For a split second, he could see past all the pretense, all the pride, and he knew he saw her, saw *her*, all that she was, and when her eyes widened in stunned shock he thought that maybe she was seeing him just as clearly.

Connor lost it. He poured himself into her, his entire body clenching and releasing with each jet. He was vaguely aware when she climaxed, her internal muscles clamping down on his surging cock. All he could do was hold on, grinding against her and filling her with everything he had.

Moments later, hours, he came to himself. With a huge amount of effort, he rolled to the side. She lay limp and quiet.

From far away a door slammed, and a voice echoed through the empty apartment. "Sorcha?"

Chapter Four

Sorcha jackknifed upright. "It's Louis." The way she said it was like the king had returned home to find the servants wearing his robes. Turning onto her knees, she felt around the small space and snatched up clothing, bundling it into her arms. With a sigh, Connor watched her stumble out of the closet. So much for afterglow.

Connor tucked himself back in his jeans, zipped up, and ambled out after her. "We've made a mess," he said. They had definitely left the closet in poorer shape than they found it. "He's going to know we've been exploring his triple Es."

Sorcha scrambled into her bra and shirt, too hurried to be graceful about it. She held up her torn panties. The fall of lace disguised the rip, but Connor knew what he had done and they were unsalvageable. Reaching over, she stuffed them in his pocket, then wriggled her skirt down around her hips. The panties burned against his leg. As did the knowledge of her naked skin underneath the skirt.

He hardened again, like a complete horndog.

"Shoo, shoo, shoo." Sorcha pushed his rear, and just because it was fun, he resisted her for a second, unyielding under her prodding. "He's not going to like it if he finds us in his bedroom either," she warned.

"I'm going to miss that closet."

"You'd miss your eyebrows a lot more. Even in human form, Louis can breathe fire when he's pissed."

She marched ahead of him down the hallway, her heels tapping in short staccatos. Her bare ass rolled under the skirt. Despite his hard-on, Connor's lips quirked.

This was shaping up to be the best day of his life. What had happened between them had been powerful, out of this world. His fantasies had built up sex with Sorcha to an amazing degree and still the reality had been better than anything he could dream up.

And they needed to talk about it. Connor wasn't one to rehash the obvious, but Sorcha could be unpredictable. Would she see the event the same way he had? More importantly, would she want to do it again?

Louis retracted from the open refrigerator, holding a bulb shaped blue bottle. His sharp gaze quickly took in Connor.

"Sorcha, how pleasant to see you. Hello, Connor. I can't say I'm as pleased to see you. Official visit, is it? Is there a problem? I can't remember doing anything criminal lately, but then again, your human laws are so confusing it's hard to keep track of what's illegal and what's only mildly offensive."

Sorcha left Connor to air kiss the vicinity of Louis's cheekbones. He wore all black, as usual, to complement the sheen of his hair. A flash of gold on his wrist and the warm brown of his skin were the only splashes of color in his monochromatic look. Wool pants creased to a knife edge brushed freshly buffed loafers.

He looked human. The only indication that he wasn't like everyone else was the blue tinge to his nails.

Louis held Sorcha at arm's length and looked her up and down. "My, my. We're a bit tarted up this evening, aren't we?"

Sorcha flushed and flicked a glance at Connor.

"Just trying something different." She tugged the hem of her skirt, as if suddenly aware of how much skin and lean, muscled leg she was showing.

"I'll say," Louis said. "If you're not careful you're going to catch a cold."

Though this was basically the same thing Connor had said earlier, he really didn't think she looked tarty, he just didn't like to share.

Sorcha huffed. "That's an old wives' tale, Louis. I could be wearing three layers and still catch a cold if the right germ got to me. Isn't that right, Connor?"

Surprised and pleased that she'd bother to ask him, as if his opinion mattered, he took his time answering. "Well, now, I don't know—"

Sorcha threw up her hands. "Oh, who cares. We have a bigger problem on our hands than my wardrobe. Can we get back on track here?"

This was fun. He spread his hands, all innocence. "I'm just saying if you were mine—"

She rounded on him. "If I was your what?"

Her ferocity surprised him. Uh-oh. It looked like somewhere he had taken a misstep, but he didn't know where. Suddenly cautious, he watched her face, wishing, not for the first time, he knew what was going on in that head of hers. "What?"

"You said if I was yours. If I was your what?" Brown eyes flashed. "Your girlfriend?"

He wasn't stupid. Connor shrugged. "Just, if you were mine."

For a moment she faltered, but gamely went on. "Well, I'm not. So," she said, turning her back on him, "Louis, here's the situation..."

While Sorcha brought Louis up to date, Connor studied her.

She seemed to be attempting to put some distance between them. It was crazy, but if he didn't know better, he'd think she was afraid. Maybe. He'd never seen Sorcha afraid before. Angry, yeah, about two dozen times, but not frightened. Of course, they'd just generated enough power to light the city for a weekend, and that certainly wasn't normal.

It scared him too, but at this point he didn't care.

Sorcha was his. Sorcha had been his for some time, he'd just been too dumb and terrified to see it. He'd wanted her, but her brazen attitude and lack of inhibition had put him off. And the truth was, maybe he'd been afraid he wouldn't be enough for her. But he could see now, he'd just been postponing the inevitable. Where Sorcha was concerned, he had no choice.

Now that he'd accepted the situation and stopped fighting himself, he was noticing some things he would have seen before if he'd been paying attention.

Sorcha had been different with him today—cold, because he'd insulted her and hurt her feelings, but with none of the taunting that usually came his way. She seemed more accessible, softer, and he thought maybe this was the real Sorcha. In a weird way, it made sense. If just being in her presence was enough to turn him into a tongue-tied tightass, then maybe being in his made her run off at the mouth.

"What are you going to do?" Louis was asking.

Sorcha lifted a shoulder. "It seems obvious Raul is the missing wyrm, wouldn't you say, Connor?"

"I hate to admit it, but yes. It's the only answer."

"Connor's been to Raul's apartment and didn't find anything."

"We could go back there and look some more," Connor said, "but I think it's a waste of time. We need to find the quickest way to stop the distribution of Bliss. Louis, you wouldn't know anything about this, would you?"

"Nope."

"You think we need to pay a visit to High Street?" Sorcha asked.

Connor nodded. "Yeah, I do. But if we go down after dark we'll have a better chance of blending in."

"Okay, it's a plan. I want to go home and change, though. If I go down to High Street looking like this it will attract the wrong kind of attention."

Connor looked her up and down. "You look beautiful," he said. "Sexy."

Her breath caught, and suddenly Sorcha looked painfully vulnerable. "I do?"

"Yeah. Too beautiful. But you know that, don't you?"

She didn't say anything, just looked at him with eyes like melted chocolate. His insides churned with heat, and something else, something he was almost ready to examine. Almost.

"I'll take you home," he said. "We need to talk."

For some reason, this made her stiffen. "Fine," she said crisply. For some reason she was avoiding his gaze, but he caught a glimpse of her eyes and saw a protective veil had been drawn.

They said their good-byes to Louis and he promised to let them know if he heard anything. Connor wasn't holding his breath. When it came to finding Raul, they were on their own.

Once in the elevator, Connor turned to her. "Sorcha?"

Sorcha wrapped her arms around her middle. She stood well over two feet away from him. The way she held herself, solitary and stiff, told him not to push her just yet.

She hardly glanced at him. "In my apartment. Please?"

After a moment he nodded. A half hour was no skin off his back. How long had they danced around each other? Years.

The past few hours had changed everything. Sorcha could pretend all she wanted, but she had been in flames for him. She wouldn't be able to go back to the way it was before, not any more than he could.

ଔଓ୫ଊଊ

Sorcha unlocked the door to her apartment. Dropping her keys into a bowl, she clicked into the kitchen. She opened the refrigerator door, knowing it was empty. A chill washed over her front as she leaned in, not seeing the yogurt, limes, brie, and racks of condiments.

"Hungry?" she asked, hoping he would say yes, but not knowing what she would feed him if he did.

"No thanks."

Still in the entryway. Good. How could she keep him there?

When he'd offered to escort her home, she'd reluctantly accepted. She'd expected he would leave and they would meet up later in the evening to go wyrm hunting. Instead, he'd stayed. To talk.

She'd prefer it if he left. What did they need to talk about? He'd wanted her, that had been obvious. Sorcha shivered involuntarily at the memory of the look in his eyes as he'd stared down at her in the closet. She'd never seen him look that way. Hot, hungry, intense. All for her. Now that he'd had her, was he done?

And what was she supposed to say? The truth wouldn't do at all. *That was the best sex I've ever had. I've loved you for years but I've been too shy to say anything.*

Not hardly. If she did, the last she would see of him would be his back as he ran for the hills, away from her, away from any sort of commitment. For males, sex was about the physical release. It was Sorcha's experience that she invested more in a relationship than the man, who liked to keep his emotions separate. No, she knew better than to mistake their closet interlude for anything other than it was—a surprise nooner.

So this talk he wanted to have—Sorcha wanted to avoid it as long as she could. But that still left Connor taking up all the air in her living space.

Suddenly it was imperative that she have a moment alone, a chance to armor herserlf. She shut the refrigerator with more force than was necessary. "I'm going to change."

Keeping to a quick walk, she ducked into the hallway. When she could see her bedroom door, her haven, she allowed a sigh. "Make yourself at home," she threw over shoulder and firmly shut the door behind her.

Leaning back against the solid door, she concentrated on its hard surface under her palms. She needed to get a grip. In that vein, a change of clothes was in order. Pushing away, she walked to her closet. The miniskirt had lost its charm long ago. Uncomfortable and foreign, it had made her feel like she was masquerading in someone else's clothes. She'd only chosen it because she'd wanted Connor to notice her. As she pulled on fresh underwear and well-worn jeans, her thoughts flashed on the time in the closet. Even the memory made her flush with heat. She'd certainly gotten her wish.

As he'd been pounding into her like a drowning man, Connor had seemed far away from the reserved lover she'd imagined him to be. Even now the memory of his hips slamming against her made her palms sweat. And she'd thought he'd be tame. Showed how much she knew.

Before she joined Connor, she stood with her hand on the knob. She found herself plucking at her necklace and dropped her hands to her sides. Tossing her hair back, she squared her shoulders, and though she wasn't nearly ready, went back to the hallway.

Connor was wandering around her living room, studying every book and picture like they were displays at a museum. As she stepped into the hall, he was leaning forward, examining a group of photos on her mantle with intense interest.

What did he think of her apartment? He'd never been here before. Somehow, she thought it was very different from how he decorated his own living space, and not just because he was a bachelor.

A muted tangerine colored the walls, contrasting with the jungle greens of the ferns and plants basking in the sunlight streaming through the windows on either side of the fireplace. An overstuffed sofa with wide teal stripes sat against the wall, in front of it a narrow coffee table that she'd draped a Mexican textile over for an additional splash of color. Books and knick-knacks were everywhere, and two bras were draped over a wooden chair with a cherry cushion where she laid them to dry.

She had grown up in a house that looked much like this one. Maybe the furniture had been a bit worn, the paint on the walls stale, but she'd inherited her mother's decorating sense along with her love of cooking. She loved her apartment and needed the bold colors like she needed air to breathe.

Standing in the middle of all the designed chaos, Connor looked like comfortable flannel. His jeans and T-shirt were faded and soft from washings, and the fabric clung to his muscles like it had been poured on. She imagined he'd go for mission style furniture, with its clean lines and uncluttered space.

"Who's this?" He indicated a picture of Sorcha with her arms wrapped around a young man, both of them flashing toothy smiles.

"My brother. I have three." She hung back in the relative safety of the hallway. One more step and she would be in his gravitational pull.

He turned, shoving lean, callused hands into his pockets. He didn't look like he wanted to run. In fact, he looked very relaxed and comfortable in her home.

"I didn't know that," he said.

"We don't know much about each other," she said softly.

"No, we don't." A second later he was in front of her, heat radiating from every pore. "Why is that, do you suppose?"

Sorcha tilted back her head. "Because you think I'm a brazen, mouthy brat, and I think you're a stuck-up prude."

If she'd thought he would be insulted, she was disappointed. He merely looked thoughtful. "Do you really think I'm a prude?"

"You don't like the way I dress, the way I talk. You disapprove of me."

"Not really."

"Do you really think I'm that unobservant? You never smile at me or initiate a conversation. If I stand too close, you turn your back. I'd say there's a problem there."

He cocked his head. “Funny,” he said, his gaze honing in on her mouth, “you don’t seem bratty or brazen now.”

“But you still disapprove.”

“Why do you keep saying that?”

Throwing up her arms, Sorcha stared at the lump of maleness in front of her in disbelief. “We had sex, Connor! In a closet! Afterwards, you don’t say anything, you don’t even touch me.”

Golden eyebrows rose. “As I recall,” he said as if picking his way through a minefield, “I wanted to talk, but you put me off. As for touching you, I wasn’t sure it was allowed.”

“Allowed! You were inside me not an hour ago. If I didn’t want you touching me, believe me, I’d have let you know before then.”

A blast of heat shot from Connor, burning her. “Do I have carte blanche to touch you anywhere I please?”

She hadn’t meant that at all, but the words of objection lodged in her throat.

“What if I wanted to touch you here?”

She watched, wide eyed, as he slid his fingertip down her cheek.

He moved on to trace the valley between her breasts. “Or here.”

She licked her lips. No. She wouldn’t let him take over again. Reaching out a steady hand she cupped the bulge in his blue jeans.

Connor surged under her hand and hissed like water on a griddle. “Sorcha,” he said through gritted teeth. “Do you have any subtlety about you at all?”

He was hard, and lengthening by the second under her palm.

"I don't think so. Is that a problem?" She squeezed him gently and was rewarded when he bucked, pushing against her palm.

"No," he managed to choke.

Her fingertip traced the outline of his hard flesh. Every bit of him was beautiful. Muscled and strong. The tip of his erection peeped out the waistband of his jeans. Her eyes about popped out of her head. Omigod, he was huge. How come she hadn't noticed that in the closet? Oh yeah, because it had been dark, and because she hadn't cared about anything other than getting him inside her as soon as possible.

His hands settled lightly on her hips, the feel so wonderful that it brought her back to reality. Were they really going to do this? Should they?

Connor McKenna wasn't for her. Not for the long term, anyway. He deserved someone *gentle* and *considerate*. Someone nice, like him. She wasn't any of these things. She was what she was, impetuous and energetic, rough and tumble, tell it like it was Sorcha. So what if he wanted her today? He had managed to avoid her for years.

Sorcha had known many men who wanted her. What she wanted was a man who stuck.

"We shouldn't do this." Her voice was husky.

Connor nuzzled her ear. "You're right. We should talk."

Absolutely not. The last thing she wanted was to talk about this, define it, put it in a box. Hear him say it was a mistake and would be over after this...after this last time.

Hooking her fingers through empty belt loops, she tugged him until the crisp hair on his lower stomach brushed lightly against her knuckles. Her fingers found the button of his jeans and with a twist the metal button popped free. Exposed, the blunt head of his erection poked through the accordion folds of his boxers.

Sorcha dropped to her knees. Urgency pounded through her and wetness rushed between her legs. He would be smooth under her tongue, spongy. If he was in her hands, between her lips, she would feel his hardness, taste the salty drops of moisture seeping from the tip.

"But—"

"Take off your shirt," she commanded.

The T-shirt whipped over his head and landed on the sofa. She rewarded him with a flick of her tongue over the smooth tip. Groaning, he bucked, then calmed enough for her to unzip his jeans and lower them so he could kick them to the side.

Sorcha sat back to see what she had uncovered. He was beautiful, all thick, sculpted muscle. His arms, chest and stomach were awash with hollows and deep shadows in the dim light. The corded muscles of his shoulders flexed as a hand stroked her hair. She could feel him looking down at her.

She knew where he wanted her to go. It was where she wanted to go, too. But he didn't push or use a grip in the tangle of her hair to guide her. He simply stood, hand resting on her hair in a gentle caress, like a god waiting his due.

Sorcha drew the tip of him between her lips, and it was like eating a plum. She drew as much as she could into her mouth. Cradled between his thighs, she lavished her feelings on the part of him that wanted her, the hard, jutting flesh rising from his stomach. She couldn't tell him she loved him, but she could stroke and lick and suck. She could tease the crinkled skin underneath and dig her fingers into the hard muscles of his thighs.

He grew to be steel, the curve of him rigid and beautiful. He smelled warm and moist, and she breathed in the scent of aroused male. His fingers tightened in her hair, tugging at her scalp, and his huge thighs trembled against her shoulders. Connor groaned, hips pushing against her in abrupt jerks, and Sorcha tasted salt. When he exploded in her mouth, she refused to release him, kept him until she knew it became uncomfortable and only then did she draw away.

Wrapping her arms around his waist, she pressed a cheek against him, burrowing into his warmth. Every second was precious, every breath she took, smelling his raw maleness, was a gift.

After a while, he gently grasped her shoulders and tried to pull her to her feet. She didn't want to go. She wanted to stay where she was. But she couldn't keep her nose in his groin forever, so she allowed him to pull her to her feet. His hands slid down her arms and their fingers entangled and he tugged. It was a signal for her to look at him. She stared at the floor.

She sat back on her haunches. How much damage had been done? How entrenched in her feelings had she become? She tried to pull her hands away. Callused fingers tightened, swallowing her own. She frowned, trying again to retrieve her imprisoned fingers.

Again, he refused to release her.

Eyes rising, she found him looking at her with an expression of such tenderness it stole the breath from her lungs. Connor's mouth widened in a slow, liquid smile. Wow, if she'd thought his frowns were amazing, his smiles were like watching the sun go nova.

He lifted her to her feet. Leaning down, he swept his lips along her jaw, light brushings. Frozen, Sorcha didn't know what to do. This tenderness was jarring, unexpected. She stood, arms held slightly out from her body, following every movement he made as if it would tell her what was going on.

He swept her up in his arms. She clutched at his shoulders. "What are you doing?"

"I'm carrying you."

A muscled, tan neck and clean cut jaw were inches from her lips. "Why?"

"Because I can. Put your arms around my neck."

He carried her to the bedroom, just like she was a freaking princess in a fairy tale. When he set her on her feet by the bed, she tried to sink onto the mattress but he pulled her upright, only pressing her back after he'd divested them of their clothing.

As he settled between her thighs, he looked down and seemed to find something in her face amusing.

"What's the matter?" he said. "Cat got your tongue?"

Frowning slightly, she shook her head. Shifting his weight onto one elbow, he reached up and massaged the vee on her forehead. After a moment, his hands slid to cup her face.

Connor brushed her temples with his thumbs. "You've driven me crazy for years." Mesmerized by green eyes, the languid brush of his voice, Sorcha floated. "I'm sorry you think I didn't like you. To tell the truth, it was deliberate on my part. You see, I was afraid if you knew I was attracted to you, you would mock me."

Mock him? Dear heaven...

"Why didn't—"

"Wait. I have another confession to make. Every time I turned my back on you? It was so I wouldn't humiliate myself. You see, even the sound of your voice is enough to make me hard. When I'm within a foot of you, well...the situation gets out of my control. You can imagine why I didn't want to advertise."

He paused as if waiting for an answer. When none was forthcoming, he bent down and licked her bottom lip.

"You're just where I've always wanted you." The scorching heat of his tongue blazed the underside of her breast. Afterward, he nibbled the same spot. "And the only reason..." nibble, nibble, "...we're not going to stay in this bed until tomorrow morning..." lick, nip, soothe, "...is because we've got a truant wyrm to find in...oh, five hours."

He drew her nipple into his mouth for a long, languid pull and Sorcha overflowed with heat. What was he doing to her? She was melting, turning into a gooey, creamy marshmallow.

And he was still talking.

"Your nipples are dark, like cherries. With your skin I should have known." A gentle puff of air puckered the nipple in question. As he bent his attention to the other one, he murmured in between licks and teasing strokes. "I've spent far too much time imagining what you looked like naked."

He progressed down her body, feasting, the mattress shifting under her with each movement. Settling between her thighs, he propped himself on his elbows and looked down at her. "Never in my wildest dreams would I have guessed you were bare down here."

She felt hot and swollen. His words, his caresses, were driving her insane. Restlessly she shifted on the bed.

"Easy. We're getting there. After all the time I spent avoiding you, I feel an imperative desire to tell you exactly how beautiful you are. Sorry," he said unapologetically. "I can't seem to shut up."

He paused and she realized he was waiting for her to say something. However, it was impossible to think past the cotton in her head, the heavy flush of her body. She couldn't say a word, couldn't even think of anything to say.

He drew a finger down her slit.

"You're wet for me even now," he said thickly. "Do you know what a turn on that is, that I've barely touched you but you're weeping for me?" Over her flushed, naked body, she watched as he brought a glistening fingertip to his lips. "Mmmm...cinnamon and musk." Connor's head dropped and the muscles in his back bunched as his shoulder blades rose. In one swipe his tongue traveled her entire slit.

Whimpering, she arched off the bed. Hard fingers gripped her hips, holding her in place. He loved her with his tongue, sweeping, probing, pausing every once in a while to turn his attention to a particular spot.

Slowly, deliberately, with his tongue and his fingers, he brought her to climax. The release spilled over her like hot chocolate, the tingling spreading from the base of her spine over her entire body. The contractions came, slow and hard, swelling to unbearable proportions.

Sorcha couldn't hold her head up any longer. Boneless, she fell back on the mattress, her heart pounding against her ribs. In the silence, she forced her head off the pillow. Connor watched her intently, eyes glowing catlike in the dark. When the last contraction melted away and her breathing no longer came in ragged gasps, he bent his head and started again.

"Oh, no. I can't possibly," she gasped.

But he ignored her, and it turned out she could.

Two more orgasms. That's what he gave her. By the end of the third, she was so exhausted she couldn't lift her head. Could only float in a daze of pleasure.

She was vaguely aware of Connor moving up her body and reaching over to fish around in her nightstand drawer. There were things in there she didn't want him to see, but when his hand withdrew, he held a foil wrapped square.

He spread her open. When he slid into her, she was soft and wet, and it was like a warm knife in butter. When he filled her completely, he kissed her, his tongue tracing her lips, coaxing her to open for him.

She could taste herself on him. His lips and around his mouth were slicked with it, as if he'd been eating a peach. As he kissed her, he began to move, the head of him retreating to the opening of her sheath, hovering there, then slamming home. Again and again, he drove into her, all the while feeding at her mouth.

The intractable, steady brush of the head of his cock over some place inside her spread ripples throughout her body. Unbelievably, she came again. As her muscles caught at the hard length inside her, Connor's movements lost some of their steadiness, and he grunted with each short, shallow stroke.

Dragging his mouth away, he sucked in a mouthful of air. He swelled uncontrollably inside her and with one last, massive thrust, ground her into the mattress.

Sorcha tightened around him, feeling great, pulsing contractions as he came. He groaned and jerked inside her. Wrapping her arms around his shoulders, her legs around his waist, she pressed him to her heart.

Tears leaked from the corners of her eyes. She didn't know why; all she could figure was she was filled with emotion and it needed a way to get out. She was able to breathe steadily only if she didn't try to stop the tears. They trickled across her cheekbone, into her ears, just one more thing she couldn't control.

She was vaguely aware Connor had rolled off because her lungs could expand again. He turned on his side and gathered her up in his arms.

Enfolded against the warm comfort of his chest, Sorcha sighed. Eyes closed, floating, she drifted off as he tucked the crown of her head under his chin. The last thing she knew was of him throwing a huge leg over hers and tugging the lower half of her body close, wrapping himself around her like an extra blanket.

Sorcha slept.

Chapter Five

When she opened her eyes, it was dark.

"Shit!" She jerked upright. At least, she tried to. Connor tightened his embrace until her nose pressed into a tangle of chest hair.

"Ow! Connor, we have to get up." Sorcha pressed ineffectually at a muscled shoulder. "We've been asleep for hours. It's night. We have to go find Raul."

Eyes squeezed shut, Connor rolled away. His shoulders took up all of her queen sized bed, the sheet bunched around his hips. "What time is it?" he mumbled.

She tore her gaze away from all the exposed flesh and glanced at the alarm clock. "Eight o'clock."

Naked, she strode into the bathroom and once the shower was heating, came back. Connor was on his stomach, face buried in a pillow, and now the view was of smoothly muscled back.

Sorcha leaned over and ran her palms down either side of his spine. His butt was tight, tighter than hers, damn him. Grabbing handfuls of lean flesh, she shook him. "Wake up."

He pushed the pillow away from his mouth. "They don't close down High Street at eight o'clock, you know. That would leave too slim a window for the drug dealers and the prostitutes to work their trade." Flipping over onto his back, he grinned at her, one eye squinted against the light from the bathroom. He slept on his stomach, and his face was puffy with sleep, the laugh lines around his eyes in greater relief.

He looked so familiar, like he'd been there a million times before, and would be for a million more.

Sorcha's heart cracked wide open at that grin. It was too much. Too much emotion, which led to too much fear. How was she supposed to handle this?

"Shower," she ground out, and fled into the bathroom.

Usually, Sorcha showered in warm water so her hair and skin wouldn't dry out. Now she turned the knob until steam filled the room in billowy clouds. Stepping under the spray, straight arms braced against the tile, she dropped her head under the searing water. It soaked her hair and ran down her back, but she barely felt it.

The tinkling of the curtain preceded a blast of cool air.

"Jesus Christ." A thick arm wrapped around her waist and pulled her from underneath the steaming deluge even as a tan hand reached to turn off the water. "Are you trying to boil yourself alive?"

Sorcha's insides churned, like she'd been drained and filled up again, only with more...more of whatever it was inside. She slumped against Connor and he took her weight against his side, gathering her hair and pulling it over her shoulder to expose her back.

Her back was hot, but his fingers were cool as they brushed softly over her skin. His palm pressed over a patch on her shoulder, fingers spread, as if he could absorb her pain with his touch. Though she wasn't really hurt, it was soothing.

"We have to take a shower," she said against his shoulder.

Dammit, Sorcha, you're not a coward. Now face what's going on and own it.

Sorcha disentangled herself from Connor, a process complicated by the fact that he wouldn't let go. Though it was like unhooking a vise, she pried his arm from her waist and turned until she could see his face.

They were both naked. She was dripping wet, and splotchy, with probably half her hair plastered to her head and the other half standing on end. No doubt she could pick a better time for her confession. But the truth filled her up, and the words needed to be said.

She tilted her head back to meet his eyes. "I love you."

His eyes honed in on hers and his whole face darkened as blood rushed to the surface of his skin. An erection brushed against her belly, hard and pulsing. Oh, lord, she could not get distracted now, and a naked and aroused Connor was enough to make her forget her own name, much less that they had a wyrm that needed saving.

Fingers flexed painfully on her upper arms.

"You're going to tell me this now? We have to go running around after Raul—who, by the way, I'm going to kiss in thanks—and you want to bare your soul?"

He didn't sound mad, though the words were spiked with sarcasm. It gave Sorcha courage.

"I've loved you for a long time," she said. "I know it's ridiculous, and I know that it will never work. But now we've...gone to bed together...the feeling is...too big. I can't hold it anymore and I needed you to know."

Sorcha was pleased to find the ball of emotion in her chest had shrunk. Now it was a burning orb the size of a baseball, not the overwhelming geyser threatening to drown her.

With a quick exhale of relief, she went to step back into the shower. Connor stopped her. “I don’t understand. Why wouldn’t we work?”

Caught naked in the fluorescent lights of the bathroom, Sorcha wanted to reach for a towel to cover herself. She felt cold, exposed.

“Well,” she said. “There are the differences between us to consider. But more importantly, you may feel desire for me, but you don’t love me.”

“But I do—”

She held out a hand. “Please. You can’t love someone after only a day in bed with them.”

“How can you—”

“Because I’ve loved you for years.”

“Sorcha, I do—”

“Connor, please, you don’t have to lie. Obviously I’ll still go to bed with you for as long as you like. My only request is you remain monogamous.”

Connor scowled. “Sorcha, I do love you, though at this moment—” With a muffled curse, he cut himself off. “Here...we don’t have time for this now.”

He pulled Sorcha to the back of the shower and with a flick of his wrist, let loose a spray of lukewarm water. After carefully adjusting the temperature, he grasped the curtain, the plastic wadded in his hand.

“I love you,” he said. “I want to climb into that shower with you and make love to you. Tonight. Tomorrow. Forever, I think. We can’t do it now, but believe me, we will. We will have this out and you are going to believe me.”

Sorcha’s heart stuttered, but she knew better than to take those hastily spoken words to heart. She reached for the shampoo. “It’s not love, Connor, it’s lust. You’re old enough to tell them apart by now.”

He gritted his teeth. “Of course I am, that’s why I’m telling you—”

Whipping around, she slammed the shampoo bottle onto the ledge. “Don’t say it again!”

For a moment, silence rang in the confined space. Sorcha wanted to cringe away from Connor’s probing gaze. She stuck her head under the water.

When she came back out, he was still there.

“Go away,” she said.

His jaw went slack and he looked at her in wonder. “You’re scared.”

She turned on him so fast the shower curtain rattled. “Of course I’m scared,” she exploded. “I’ve never been in love before. I don’t think I like it.”

“You think I’m not terrified? That I don’t wonder if you’ll wake up a week from now and decide you need someone more exciting?”

She scrubbed ferociously at her scalp. “That’s ridiculous,” she snapped. “What kind of an idiot wouldn’t find you exciting?” Soap slid down her forehead and she tilted her head back to protect her eyes. “One day, Connor, you’ll come to your senses and realize I’m too undisciplined for you. You’ll walk away and I’ll…I’ll…”

Be alone. Without even the hope that Connor might love her back.

“I’m not going anywhere,” he said with calm assuredness. “I’m a prize idiot for not letting you know how I felt sooner. But all this time hasn’t been wasted. Maybe it took us this long to figure out what we wanted." Green eyes pinned her. "I want you."

Sorcha stared at him, fingers buried in her sudsy hair, bubbles stinging the corners of her eyes. Wrenching away, she shoved her face under the spray. Completely rinsed, she turned, mouth open. She knew exactly what she was going to say.

Unfortunately, when she pulled back the curtain and looked around the bathroom, he was gone.

ଔଓଛଡ଼

He hadn't gone far, just to the bedroom. When Sorcha was done, Connor showered while she dressed in black jeans and a black, v-necked shirt. Apparently, the conversation was over.

Well, Sorcha thought, feeling sulky. Good.

"We need to go by my apartment to get my gun," Connor said.

Guardians were trained for hand-to-hand combat and to handle firearms. Wyrms often found themselves in situations where extraction was necessary. Babysitting duties were the day-to-day. Bodyguard duties came on-line when the babysitting failed. Their duty wasn't to protect the wyrms, it was to protect humans.

"I hate wyrms," Sorcha said, arming herself. "Why can't we just pump them full of drugs or something?"

"We haven't found one that stays in their system longer than five minutes."

"Right." And killing them outright was out of the question.

"That's why we're here. No one can control the wyrms. We just have to stay close and do the best we can to make sure they stay out of trouble."

Sorcha sighed. "When this is over, I think I'll retire. Louis is petulant and selfish, and when he acts like we were put on this earth for his pleasure it makes me want to scream."

"I've wanted to quit for years," Connor said quietly. "I only stayed because of you." He stuffed his wallet into his pocket. "That's probably why I haven't been as attentive to Raul as I should have been lately. The whole thing is beginning to feel like a chore."

Sorcha nodded, once again struck speechless. That was exactly how she felt. "A chore."

But was it true? Had he only stayed as a Guardian because of her? It was hard to believe, but Connor had spoken calmly and matter-of-factly. It had sounded like the truth.

If it was...

What? Would she throw herself at him and suddenly believe everything would be okay? No way. He didn't love her. And he hadn't stayed around just for her, whatever he thought. He'd probably stayed because of Cisco.

Her heart might tell her to believe him, but her heart was a fool. And it wanted to believe what he was saying. It flared like a star when he'd said he loved her. But her heart wanted things it couldn't have. She couldn't trust it, could only trust what her mind told her was the truth. Men didn't love Sorcha Jimenez. They may love her body, they may welcome her into their lives for a while, but in the end she was never enough for them.

Or maybe she was too much.

Either way, it was better for both of them if she acted like she'd never heard the words.

Chapter Six

Connor didn't like the way the punk with the blade-thin mustache and neck tattoo was looking at Sorcha.

Lids slitted with lusty appreciation, the youth ran his gaze over her breasts for the third time. Connor wanted to punch him. Still, he couldn't really blame him. Sorcha truly was sex walking. He sighed. Might as well get used to it. Sorcha wouldn't hide under a basket because he was jealous of every man with a pair of eyes in his head, and he didn't want to ask her to.

There would be no punching today. They needed this punk. It had taken two hours of trolling High Street, posing as a couple out for a good time, to get a bite on the Bliss. He looked around at the slimy street, the broken bottles and trash washed against the side of buildings. Connor hated going to High Street. Afterwards, he always felt as if he needed a steam clean.

It had rained while he and Sorcha slept, bringing a wave of humidity to the city. The air was heavy and smelled like steamed pavement. Not even weeds bothered to poke through the cracks in the sidewalk. Even in spring, High Street was dirty and depressing.

The guy in front of him was just a kid, scrawny arms falling out of a white basketball jersey, baggy pants shoved low on his hips. However, he had enough attitude for ten people. "If I were with you, *chica*," he said, "I wouldn't need any pharmaceutical to get my motor running, if you know what I mean." He palmed his sagging crotch and hefted himself. Connor took a step forward, his shoulders tensed and ready for battle. He was going to pull the kid's ball sac out his nose.

A hand on his arm stopped him. Sorcha turned back to the street punk. "Flattering. Do you have the Bliss or not?"

Connor held his temper. This scrawny meerkat, overinflated with his own self-importance, would lead them to Raul. Meerkat was a small cog, but now they'd found him, Raul wasn't far behind. They just needed to be patient.

"I got it. I got it. Chill," Meerkat said. "You got the Benjamins for a shot?"

"How much?" Connor said.

"Five."

Connor wasn't surprised at the amount, but the guy he was pretending to be would be. "Five! You gotta be kidding me. For how much?"

"One night, bro."

"Why should I pay that much for a hard-on?"

Meerkat shrugged. "You're the one came looking. Look, man, this stuff is complex. You'll be like this," he clenched his scrawny fist, "all night long. It'll make *la bonita chica* very happy."

Cursing, Connor put on a big show, stalking away, muttering to himself. Trailing after him, Sorcha placed her hand on his arm and leaned in to whisper, "We got him. Let's go call the Director." From a distance, it would look like she was urging him to pay the cash.

Meerkat smirked at them—two suckas with more money than sense.

"All right," Connor said. "I guess it's worth it." He made the mistake of glancing at Sorcha, who smiled brilliantly and shoved her chest two inches forward, as if it would persuade him to make the right decision. Connor couldn't help but smile back, but when he remembered he wasn't the only one looking at her, he lapsed into a scowl. She winked.

He turned back to Meerkat. "Where is it?"

Slitted eyes became crafty. "I don't have it, man. We have to wait for my...supplier."

"It better not take long," Connor said, allowing very real tension to creep into his tone. "I don't have all night."

"For sure, guy."

So they waited. And waited some more. Connor considered walking away. Meerkat was definitely the supplier of Bliss, at least at the street level. Meerkat didn't have Raul tucked in his back pocket, but he was a link, and one link was all they needed.

Footsteps moved gravel behind him and Meerkat's eyes focused on something.

"It took you long enough," Meerkat said. "I thought I'd have to take this guy out myself."

Connor whipped around to find Sorcha imprisoned by a huge guy wearing paint stained pants and an old leather jacket gaping around his huge gut. This guy was older than Meerkat but didn't look as cunning. One arm was wrapped around her neck, the other cinched under her breasts, pulling her back tight against his bulk.

Connor lunged for Sorcha but stopped dead when he saw the flash of a gun barrel in the light.

"I wouldn't." The big guy pressed the round barrel under her ear. "Or, whatever. Go ahead. It won't stop anything."

Meerkat stepped forward, smirking. “Yeah, guy. She’s going with us. We’ve got a dose of Bliss set aside just for her. She’s gonna make a lot of customers very happy tonight. Too bad it won’t be you.”

Fuck. Connor’s gaze centered on the gun. He was close enough to see the barrel depress her skin. When removed, a round mark would remain. He focused on the abomination of the cold steel at her throat, forgetting, for the moment, that Meerkat even existed.

A weight exploded in his skull. As he fell to the wet pavement, Sorcha’s horrified gaze followed him down. The last thing he saw was a large hand anchoring her wrists, then the other covering her throat.

ঌ৫ঌ৫

Before he pried his lids open, Connor was searching for his cell phone. He located its hard shape in his pocket. Thank God he’d brought it with him. He was never leaving the house without one again.

Idiots. Dead idiots when he got to them.

He was strangely cold and calm, his emotions frozen. That was good. He needed to be able to function. How long had he been out? Not long. In this part of town, you could be stripped of your clothes and fillings in under a minute.

Connor heard a creaking, like plastic nearing the fracture point, and realized he had the phone in a death grip. He forced himself to relax his fingers. But the second of calm produced a thawing in the ice that held him level. Sick panic clawed his breastbone.

Sorcha. They were going to shoot her full of Bliss and sell her to the highest bidder. Godammit, he should have known.

The Director answered his direct line.

"Sorcha. They've got her," Connor said without preamble.

After a second's pause. "Where are you?"

"High Street. We found the runner who was selling the Bliss, but they took Sorcha. They plan on dosing her up on Bliss and declaring open season."

Nausea sat thick in his throat, and every muscle was taut. Calm. He needed to calm down. He couldn't save her if he was insane with fear. *Don't think about what could be happening. Don't imagine Sorcha shot full of drugs, at the mercy of some faceless, horny old toad who only wanted to...*

Through a roaring haze, the Director was speaking.

"...and we'll follow the GPS signal on her phone. It will lead us right to them. Don't worry, Connor."

Whatever. There were no worries. He was going to kill anyone who laid a finger on his woman.

ଔଓ୫ଚ୫ଚ

"Go ahead and stick her."

The skinny guy was watching her, anticipation bright in his eyes.

"The boss told me not to," said the big guy. The one holding a gun to her side.

"How's he gonna to know?"

The big guy wasn't the sharpest tool in the shed, but he wasn't being given enough credit. "She'll be humping the walls by the time we get there. You don't think they'll notice that? Come on, Geo, they'll know."

Geo threw himself back in the seat, arms crossed over his narrow chest. "I want to see what this stuff does. What does it matter? We could have some fun and nobody would know."

She wanted to point out that she couldn't have sex with two men and there not be any effects from it. The next man, the man who'd paid for her, would definitely know. There'd be marks on her skin, elsewhere on her body, all signs she wasn't "fresh".

But the big guy couldn't articulate all that, so he just said, "We don't stick her."

Well, this was just great. She was riding down High Street in the back of a Cadillac with two low rent street thugs riding herd on her.

She'd underestimated them, or more likely, their boss. It had never occurred to her they would use Bliss to turn innocent women into sex-starved love slaves. It was brilliant. Twisted, but brilliant.

She bided her time, intensely aware of the gun digging into her ribs. After a short time the car squeaked to a halt. They were still on High Street, parked outside a hulking, derelict warehouse.

Sorcha didn't pay much attention to her surroundings as they pushed her inside. She was more interested in catching her kidnappers in a weak moment. She watched them carefully, her attention never wavering as she waited for her chance. They opened the door to a room containing a tarnished brass bed, a dresser, and a mirror. The walls were concrete and a naked bulb hung low from the ceiling.

Sorcha took in all the dinginess. They hadn't even attempted to transform the room. It was a concrete box with a huge mirror positioned so that whoever was on the bed got an eyeful of themselves. Ick. If they were expecting anyone to have sex in this room, they were going to have to give the guy some Bliss, too.

In the doorway, she tensed, but Geo pushed her forward and she stumbled. She gained her feet and whipped around. They had followed her into the enclosed space and blocked the door.

"Too bad it wasn't to be between us. Don't cry. If you want, Geo will come around after your date and make it right. Geo doesn't mind sloppy seconds."

Sorcha sized up the room, looking for anything she could use as a weapon. "Does Geo mind being a eunuch?"

He laughed. "So brave now, aren't you, *chica*? I'll be back in a few hours. Let's see if you're feeling so smart then."

In one hand, he flashed a pair of handcuffs. Where had he gotten them? When? They jingled coldly, another shade of industrial in the stark room. He advanced on her, the big guy flanking her other side. They meant to handcuff her to the bed.

Vaulting up onto the mattress, she kicked off her shoes and pressed herself into the angle of the walls. It was hardly a position of strength, but it would have to do. Fortunately, her move surprised her attackers. Instead of rushing her as they should have, they checked up.

She jerked her cell from her pocket and jabbed at the buttons.

"Hey!" Geo lunged. A second later, so did the big guy.

Sorcha kicked, but the mattress was thin and she couldn't gain purchase. Her bare foot connected to Geo's shoulder. Hardly stunned, he yanked an ankle out from under her. Flailing, she went down, her head connecting with the headboard.

Next thing she knew, she was attached to it.

Curled around her handcuffed hand, she recoiled into the wall. Geo loomed, holding her cell in one hand and a needle a mile long in the other.

“Fight me now, bitch. Because after a dose of this, you’ll be begging me to take you down.”

Her head fell back, lids drifting shut, as if she were having trouble remaining conscious. He should have had the big guy hold her legs. He should have kept his distance. But he was inexperienced and distracted, and when he leaned down, she head-butted him, aiming for the softest place on his face.

With a shriek, he jerked backwards, dropping the phone. Blood spurted over his white jersey from his nose. The big guy immediately went to help him, but Geo swatted him off and tugged the gun from the back of his waistband.

“Bitch!”

The gun rose, and the black, gleaming weight pulled at the skinny arm trying to hold it steady.

Geo aimed between her eyes. She knew he wasn’t supposed to shoot her. Alive, she would make his boss money tonight. All he had to do was inject a little Bliss in her veins, and his job would be complete. But she’d insulted his manhood by getting the better of him and she could tell by the hard set of his jaw and his agitated movements that he was no longer thinking of what his boss wanted.

Sorcha’s breathing reduced to jerking pants.

The big guy reached for the gun. Geo whirled and shot him in the foot.

Stunned, Sorcha shrank from the man howling on the floor, his wounded appendage clutched as close as his girth would allow. The gunshot echoed through the confines of the concrete room, mixing with the screams.

Geo turned back to Sorcha.

"Beg me. *Beg me, chica,* and I may let you live."

Oh, Connor... she thought, numb with panic and sadness.

If she hadn't been such a scaredy-cat, she'd have months', years' worth of memories with Connor to treasure, instead of one. God, couldn't she respect him enough to believe he knew his own mind? If Connor said he wanted her, then he wanted her.

The anger she felt at her own ridiculous fear gave an edge to her voice.

"Go to hell."

"You think I won't kill you?"

"Your boss wouldn't like it."

"My boss won't give a damn. An hour back on the streets and I can get one just like you, ten more of you if I had to. You're nothing."

There was nothing else to say. Needlessly provoking him was suicide and she wasn't ready to die. Not in this crummy, nasty room in this crumbling warehouse. Especially not after what had happened with Connor, and the possibility, given time, oh please God, of what could happen still.

Footsteps pounded in the corridor. Sorcha held her breath, eyes glued to the wavering gun barrel. Geo's arm shook. When he'd chosen a firearm, he had not chosen wisely. He'd gone for the biggest, the deadliest looking, and he was struggling.

His arm would give out soon, but before it did, he would shoot her just for the hell of it.

The door burst open.

"Sorcha!"

Connor barreled into the room, eyes wild, hair flying. He didn't bother to look where he was going, didn't stop to take stock of the situation. Eyes locked on her, he propelled past Geo and threw himself at her, taking her down to the mattress.

"No!" she cried, struggling against the weight of him. He covered her, and she pushed frantically at his shoulders. "Get away. He's going to shoot."

He pressed her down into the moldy cotton pad until she couldn't see, couldn't breathe. Could only whisper prayers underneath the heavy beat of pounding feet.

After a few disorienting minutes, Connor raised himself. A handcuffed Geo was being led from the room, which was full of Directorate. Someone handed Connor a tiny key and he unlocked the handcuff. Sorcha pressed her wrist against her stomach, rubbing at the reddened skin.

Connor picked her up by the shoulders and shook her. "Are you okay?" He dragged her to his chest and squeezed the breath out of her. "You scared me half to death."

Rough, large hands were everywhere, scanning her body for bruises or wounds. When he got to her head, he growled.

She giggled, a little desperately. "You should see the other guy."

"Not funny. Definitely not funny. Do not laugh or I'll spank you."

Her mouth fell open. "Why?"

"If you hadn't insisted on coming with me this never would have happened."

That was so unfair Sorcha didn't know what to say. They worked for the same company, didn't they? Could he have turned his back on their job, on Raul?

A great shudder rippled through Connor's chest. "I've never been so scared in my life," he whispered. Sure enough, his heart raced, and the huge paw scraping her hair was trembling.

Was this really happening? Would she allow herself to be vulnerable, open to pain and disappointment? Connor certainly seemed game to take her on, all of her, and he certainly knew her drawbacks better than anyone.

Connor buried his face in her neck.

She lifted a hand, fingers hovering over golden hair. Hesitating only a moment, they slid into the thick strands.

With a rumble of approval, Connor settled her more firmly against him. His lips pressed to her fluttering pulse.

Sorcha might be slow, but she always learned from her mistakes. Nothing on this earth would tear her from Connor's side, not as long as he loved her. She'd trust him, trust him to know his feelings. Trust him not to dick around with hers.

Scary, yes. But scarier yet not to be with him at all.

ଔଓ୫ଌ

After that, finding Raul proved anticlimactic.

He was in a room much like the Sorcha's, only bigger, with cushions and purple gauze attached to the walls. It was very harem/prison chic.

Naked, Raul reclined amongst the pillows like a pasha. A flat screen TV played Spanish soap operas, and a room service cart with the remains of a lavish meal and several empty bottles of champagne sat in the corner. Between his legs, a naked woman was busy procuring the next installment of Bliss.

"Connor, what are you doing here?" Raul said, sounding none too pleased. The girl between his legs stroked away.

At first sight of Raul, Connor grasped Sorcha's shoulders and turned her face to the wall.

"Rescuing you," Connor said, an edge of sarcasm biting through as he quickly got the gist of the situation.

"Well, could you come back and rescue me in about two days? I should be tapped out by then."

Disgusted, Connor turned around and walked out, hand clasped tightly to Sorcha's. He walked down the hall, striding toward the Director who was talking with a group of men in vests and gear, one of whom was Cisco.

He brushed past the Director's shoulder, not even looking at him.

"We quit."

The Director stopped his conversation and watched them walk down the hall. "Sorcha. Is that right?"

Sorcha adjusted her grip on Connor's hand, leaning against the solid length of him. This was the kindest, sexiest man on the planet and she loved him.

She looked up into Connor's emerald gaze.

"Consider us resigned."

Connor grinned and pressed a kiss on her knuckles.

Cisco's comment caught them at the door.

"It's about time."

About the Author

Nina Mamone grew up in the mountains of West Virginia. After she discovered Nancy Drew, she could always be found in a corner with her nose in a book. Now she lives with her husband and daughter, writing in between looking at piles of laundry and being a stay-at-home mom.

If you'd like to contact her, send an email to ninamamone@yahoo.com.

Printed in the United Kingdom
by Lightning Source UK Ltd.
133124UK00001B/228/A

9 781599 983653